BROKEN WING SPARROW

Broken Wing Sparrow

Mary Buford

iUniverse LLC
Bloomington

BROKEN WING SPARROW

This is a work of fiction. All of the characters, names, incidents, organizations, and dialogue in this novel are either the products of the author's imagination or are used fictitiously.

iUniverse books may be ordered through booksellers or by contacting:

iUniverse LLC
1663 Liberty Drive
Bloomington, IN 47403
www.iuniverse.com
1-800-Authors (1-800-288-4677)

Because of the dynamic nature of the Internet, any web addresses or links contained in this book may have changed since publication and may no longer be valid. The views expressed in this work are solely those of the author and do not necessarily reflect the views of the publisher, and the publisher hereby disclaims any responsibility for them.

Any people depicted in stock imagery provided by Thinkstock are models, and such images are being used for illustrative purposes only.
Certain stock imagery © Thinkstock.

Original art work by E. C. Dotson
Credits go to: Teri Richards/Willow Valley Photography

ISBN: 978-1-4917-3613-5 (sc)
ISBN: 978-1-4917-3676-0 (e)

Library of Congress Control Number: 2014909944

Printed in the United States of America.

iUniverse rev. date: 06/04/2014

I dedicate this book to . . .

My daughter
My husband
My family & friends
All the religious clergy
Everyone reading this book

Thank you for all you've given me! God bless!

CHAPTER 1

I remember that night, well bits and pieces anyway; as slowly by more definitely, I am losing what I have of my past memory. In fact, I can't even remember some of my own memory that goes onto paper here today, unless I go back and re-read it, as I have already done so several times. Earlier that day, the day in question, I had a wedding to celebrate; well I wasn't celebrating with the bride & groom, I was their priest, celebrating the mass. The day was a beautiful one to remember, with the flowers, limos, and all the trimmings. I remember not being able to attend the reception as I was preparing for a funeral, a man who had attended the church; I called home; his whole life. It would be one of the largest and most influential funeral sermons I was ever to give; and I needed to be prepared for it. I had only been a priest for 15 years, and I even graduated early in my class. I knew the day I wanted to be a priest, the day that I received my calling, although I was now losing that memory, along with all other memories surrounding it.

The weather report said that there would be clouds in the sky all day, but no one predicted the late day fog that would come, along with the thunderstorm to arrive even later. It was the kind of weather that you make a pot of tea, or if you find yourself feeding those who don't wish to go out in that type of weather, you find your biggest pot and make chili. That type of weather isn't usual typical weather for this time of year in Wisconsin - the dairy state, the land of milk and honey. It was all so odd that day, with the weather acting in the way that it did; but sometimes I guess that's just the way life goes, or so I'm told.

After getting the sermon written in the church for the funeral the next day, I remember feeling the hunger that reminded me that I had long-overlooked both, lunch and supper. I suppose when you know you are delivering the sermon at one of the largest funerals in the state, it's easy to get all caught up in what to say. Luckily I was done with figuring out what direction in which to take my sermon, and I had saved the manuscript to my laptop. I remember leaving the church and locking up behind me. It had raining just a bit, but nothing too harsh. I figured if I hurried back to the rectory, I might just make it without getting too wet. The rains started up again as I was on my way back to the old rectory, where I shared living space with 6 other priests and 2 bishops, along with 4 retired priests. Upon getting closer to the rectory, it started to rain harder. I didn't have my umbrella, as I was in a hurry that morning, as I had overslept. I had been up all night getting ready for the wedding ceremony that day before, and then awoke in the night with one of those dreams that makes you wish you weren't a priest, at least not a celibate one. The kind of dream that you wished would just somehow pass you by. The rain only continued to get harder and fall faster, and soon it was starting to hail, small and light at first, then get heavier and harder. I pulled my trench coat up over my head to prevent injury from the hail, but when that didn't fare well for me, I decided to lift my attaché' over my head and walk faster. Thunder clashed around me as I continued to walk home, it was thundering all around me, as if someone was in the back alley kicking old metal garbage cans. It was loud! My dress shoes pounded the wet pavement faster and faster, as I could see the outside light on at the rectory. It cut through the darkness like the beacon of light at sea. It was obvious that the housekeeper had noticed my absence during the evening meal when she was serving the others in the rectory. I don't know what happened next, but I remember the pain, in my arms and legs as I fell to the ground. There was a sharp feeling in my chest that wouldn't allow me to keep with my breathing. Someone or something was near me. No face, no form, but someone. I felt at peace, and wondered if this was the end of this life. It was becoming more and more difficult to breathe, until I blacked out. I heard nothing. I felt nothing.

I came to in the hospital. It was a clean-smelling environment with white everywhere, floors, sheets, walls. At first I didn't even know where I was. I heard voices to my left, and looking in that direction, I noticed Bishop Donald Hein was standing out in the hall talking with a doctor or nurse trying to make sense of it all. I didn't know who the other male voice was. It didn't really matter. I looked down to see what kind of shape I was in. I noticed that I was connected to an IV-line, and could hear my heartbeats through the machine that the sticky probes were connected to. I had no idea what happened. No remembrance of what had happened. No understanding of what was going on. The last thing I remembered was walking in the hail storm that had come from out of nowhere, all so sudden. I noticed on the side of the bed was a notebook. It was open to a certain page of manuscript. It looked like my handwriting. It read:

Yesterday they told me that I could remember more than I could today, leaving out a visit from someone as I lay helpless on the sidewalk. I don't remember that now. I can't remember the name of the man who's funeral I was preparing for, even though I should be able to, one would think; nor do I remember the wedding that took place earlier that day, only to say that there was one; and I do remember a few bits and pieces, however I am expecting to lose those sometime in the near future. I don't even remember what the condition is called that I have, even though I remembering someone sharing that with me at some point.

Oh, wow, did that say a lot. I now remembered briefly the wedding, and the upcoming funeral that was to come. I imagine as I am lying here in the hospital, more things will come to mind. How long had I been awake, and why don't I remember waking up before? How bad this condition must be, or how bad off am I?

Bishop Hein returned from the hallway with a look of gloom in his eyes. Knowing it couldn't be good, I had to ask.

What did they tell you? I asked him as he came into the room.

His reply was simple, *they tell me that this will only get worse, and you may not even remember being a priest one of these days!*

How can that be? I was concerned. I enjoyed being a priest; oh sure, I could do without those temptation dreams, but even Jesus was lead into the desert. Being a priest was all I knew, and hopefully I didn't lose that part of my memory. If I wasn't a priest, what was I? The vows that I took meant so much to me. Would I just forget to deny my own vows? This was something that I worried about as he told me more:

Doctors tell me that you could lose all of your memory, back to childhood even if the swelling on the brain doesn't stop. No two brain injuries are the same, no matter the similarities in the injury. I understand it is affecting the declarative and non-declarative parts of your memory. Now I don't expect you to remember that, because tomorrow I MAY NOT remember that, but please know that we, the clergy of the Catholic Church, are here for you as you heal. St. Michael's church, your parish, will be watched over by Father Lucas Jameson; a new priest looking to get some more experience with the mass; so take your time; and we are all praying for you. If you need to take some additional time off to get to know your surroundings better, now is a good time. We understand. We are all praying. God Bless Father!

He was clearly upset. He left the hospital room with no more to say. I suppose it wouldn't do much good, as I probably wouldn't remember it anyway. We didn't need to have any more shortage of priests, as we were already getting priests from other parts of the world just to save our own souls in America. I was so happy to answer that call, but who's to say that it's going to be easy for me if or when I lose that part of my memory. It wasn't easy to look into his face that day, that part I do remember vividly. I may not remember the conversations prior to that, however, the look on his face I will never forget. He had a solemn look on his face. His eyes were deep set and dark. He looked as though he had been up all night in prayer. Later that night as I lay awake waiting for the medicine to take its toll on my system, awaiting sleep; I could still remember his face, his look, even though some of his words were becoming less clear. Without hearing their conversation in the hall earlier that day, somehow I knew it was going to get worse, somehow I just knew, and that look on Bishop Hein's face was all the proof I needed, that was all I needed to know.

Saturday, May 05, 2012

The next day was much the same, re-reading over all the papers that I had written on Catholic theology, I felt mostly the same about who I was then and now, none of that had changed as of yet, but I couldn't remember some of my schooling, the classes, the teachers/clergy were getting fuzzy in my mind. I was writing things down, and not sure how to handle it all.

I was a strong believer in God, Jesus, the Holy Spirit, and the Bible; yet nothing could give me strength today, nothing really set the standard for me, and that was so unlike me; I was beginning to get scared.

Who would I become if I wasn't a priest.... Where would I live?

Thoughts of church teachings danced in my mind, without that I'm just not me, I thought... or so I thought! Perhaps Bishop Hein had some answers for me, as he seemed to for everyone else; but the look on his face just a day before still lingered in my mind, as I lingered in thought.

Just at that point the thought that changed everything entered my mind...

What was God's plan for me? Was this all part of the larger plan?

Those questions would take over all other thoughts at this point, as I soon came to understand that what had happened that night had to do with lightening. Storms and lightening are acts of God, like it or not. Perhaps He was giving me new direction in which to live, but *what could be a more honorable way of life than to be a priest?* Thoughts danced over and over throughout my mind throughout the day, as visitors no longer came once they knew I was alright, well almost alright. I suppose everyone knew I had to be in prayer more and more, and more and more would I rely on the prayer book than memory. I began to pray...

Oh God, whose only begotten Son, by His life, death, and resurrection has purchased for us the rewards of eternal life, grant, that we beseech Thee, that meditation upon these mysteries in the most Holy Rosary of the Blessed Virgin Mary, we may imitate what they contain, and obtain what they promise: through the same Christ our Lord. Amen.

I was struck by lightning!

The thought interrupted my prayers.

Oh Father in Heaven - I was struck by lightning! That's an act of God! Father, I hear you reaching to me; and I am ready to answer your call for more than I thought you wanted me for!

I was reaching to Him in spirit. He was the answers and the reason for my prayers. He was the reason for my existence. He made sure that I was okay through the storm, and made sure that he sent someone to help me, probably the clergy. Just as I was once called upon to be a priest, he was now calling me to behold myself into something more; and more than I could even understand. You see, I find that understanding God is like putting together a puzzle; we only hold one piece at a time, and are not given the big picture of our lives until the very end. Perhaps we do see smaller versions of the big picture, or smaller pieces of what is to come, at those right times in our lives. Oh how holy the man that gets called twice to serve our Heavenly Father! I was lucky enough to be paid attention to by Our Lord and Heavenly Father. I was lucky enough to recognize God working with me again and again! Now, this was going to be the ultimate calling, if there is such a thing; I was glorifying myself thinking I was the lucky chosen one. How lucky could I be, if I couldn't grasp much memory anymore? I would try for Him and for myself.

CHAPTER 2

Upon coming home, I went through an angry faze, nothing to be concerned about, but in reality, I was angry for what happened to me. Oh sure, I know I was accepting the fate Our Lord had set for me, but why was it ME? I mean, I had so much to do, and so very little time to do it in. I didn't understand half of what I was supposed to, and the most frustrating part of this entire situation was that I was a good priest. In the paper this morning I heard of a priest in a scandal, and I instantly was bothered by that. Not only could he remember everything, he chose not to! I mean, really. If you did something wrong, it's obvious that you should admit fault and move forward. If not, then pray that the world knows you are innocent. Here I am in the mist of all this work that needs to be done, and I can't even do it! Really? I don't have the memory to do my own job, and then there are those that make a mockery of the white collar, whether it is the priest or the accuser. The more I thought about it, the more upset I became. I was in my room at the rectory, when pure anger struck! I don't know that I threw a fit like this before, but I know I was ready to release anger now! My books and papers from the seminary were stacked neatly on the shelf. I picked them up and screamed out loud to them.

How could this happen to me? I wanted to know why this didn't happen to a priest who needed to be re-vamped into a better priest! Why me? I have so much work to do, some I don't even remember how to, and some I don't even remember writing down. The part that really bothers me is the lack of answers! Please answer me, give me some kind of direction.

I set the papers back on the shelf and sat on the edge of my bed. I didn't know what to think or what direction my life was going, so I started to cry. Imagine a priest, the one who is taught to console, crying as if he were a baby! Oh, how I needed some direction. I needed a friend. I needed God.

Weeks went by and I lost most of my memory, at least that part of it anyway. I remembered the childhood stuff, like not liking cherry-flavored Kool-Aide, but then forgetting some of what I had previously written in my days at the seminary. Now re-reading those writings, it was like going to school all over again. Not only was I surprised by what I wrote, I wasn't even sure if I believed in it anymore. Some of the teachings still made sense to me; but most was more of confusion. I was starting to question things like celibacy and the priesthood; which was more annoying, as I know these were not questions in my head earlier. I remembered that I was a virgin, and was grateful that those intimate thoughts still lay intact in my head, and not ever acted upon. The temptations were gone; however more questions remained; especially as more discoveries were opened in my thoughts, though the answers in my mind were diminishing.

Why don't priests marry?

Why do priests live solitary lives?

Why couldn't we hold a beautiful woman that God created in our arms, in a warm, loving, caring embrace and entangle our arms around each other as though we were going to hold on forever?

Why was it so difficult for me to remember those years in the seminary, but I can remember the useless menu from yesterday...and I can still smell the homemade bread from down on the farm?

What's important to remember and what is not?

I no longer had just those questions, but I was losing the purpose behind the questions too!

Later that day, the President for the Rosary Making Society Group, Tammy Peters, stopped by with a bag full of rosaries. I loved the rosary, and was always grateful for the handcrafted rosaries from anyone in the parish. It was difficult to talk with her, as she knew things were not so right with me. Her eyes filled with tears as I no longer remembered what I would say to bless the beautiful rosaries she brought, so I gave them a generic blessing and hoped she wouldn't mind. There was purpose in her life now, and I almost envied her for it. She was a single mother, heavyset middle-aged woman, who was raising her teenage daughter alone in the world, with little to no help from her family. She had been through a lot in her life, and I remember being there as a shoulder to cry on for her. She didn't have much to spare but would take any and all left over money to purchase rosary parts and beads to get more prayers out into the world. Today I saw her for her inward beauty and thought how God really did a good job with her soul. I don't know how I had normally felt for her, but today I could see inside and was pleased with the work of God. I remembered, actually remembered, that I had the pleasure of getting to know her personally while helping her with her annulment paperwork. Her husband had been mistreating her, emotionally and physically. It was clear later during the marriage, the abuse she endured, that had crept into her life, was there to stay, as if settling itself in, and becoming worse and worse. She didn't see it coming, nor did she ask for much in return. He was a greedy man who would take from her and their daughter as often as he could, often times taking money out of the bank after her direct deposit. They rented a run-down shack, formerly a gas station on the outside of town. I saw bruises and deep sadness on her face one Sunday, and asked what wrong. She hadn't wanted to share with me, because she didn't feel as though she should talk bad about the man she was married to. I finally pushed the issue a bit harder, for her and her daughter's sake; and I'm sure glad I did, as I was able to get her the help she needed. She was able to stay in a home for abused families, and I further had her connected to a Christian therapist, a divorced-Catholic support-group, a divorce attorney (yes, those are necessary sometimes), and finally her annulment paperwork and process, which was granted almost instantly. I saw some of his abuse first hand. Not only did I report it to the police, but I also sent copies of the police reports to the Tribunal office of our Diocese, with whom she was going through for the annulment. I have seen all kinds of women pass through the divorce/annulment stage. Some are reluctant and end up waiting for years for the annulment. Other times, rarely, but it happens that the wife goes back to the abuser husband. I had personally seen a couple of cases first hand. In one case he got the help he needed and gave her a happy home to come home to; however, in the other case, I was present to see more abuse come to a wife after she left her husband, then went back to him. The abuse from that case grew and grew, until one day I answered the phone to find that he had killed her. The abuse only stops when the abuser ends it. There is little to do if the one receiving the abuse doesn't walk away. No one can help unless help is the only option. I was glad that Tammy went through that storm as though she were ready for it. I would imagine she could endure no more; there was no doubt in my mind. I was so proud of her accomplishments, including, but not just, all the work she was doing for the church. Her daughter is a very loyal and devoted server of my parish, often times meeting me at the door as I was arriving to be prepared for the day's mass. The daughter, a happy-go-lucky simple teen girl, was going to be happy with whomever her mother would select to lead their small family to church, if/when God made it appropriate in their lives. They were strong and quite possibly ready for that next chapter one day. I found myself thinking how they really deserved the best man for the job, whoever he may be. Tammy would make a wonderful wife, again for a Catholic gentleman someday. Perhaps she would be granted that, and for that I prayed for her, while I still had the memory to remember how.

I would see her more often, when her work schedule would allow. I felt as though she was inspiring me to improve my memory by bringing me books and magazine articles on memory loss, head injuries, and testing skills and abilities reviews that she found on-line somewhere. I was pleased to know that God was helping her help me. She obviously didn't forget all that I had helped her with, and now that she was free from the abuser, I was wondering if God planned on directing her back in my path. Perhaps it was my turn to listen to those around me instead of listening to the inner voice in my head. Maybe instead of having to find the great words of wisdom, it was time to reflect in echoing silence. Perhaps the time had come that with all thoughts, purposes, and desires; God would work through me before putting me back on track, into the priesthood once again. I was hopeful that I would wake up one day and it would all be right there, at my fingertips. I wanted back behind the altar again, and I was prayerful and hopeful that it would happen again for me one day. It's obvious after all that I had been through that the Lord works in mysterious ways, no doubt. Here I was, helpless in a hospital, finally coming to the realization that I didn't know it all. My sister Lili would be so proud, reminding me that I didn't know it all through-out our childhood days. Ah, my sister would so have fun with me now, if leaving to a different state wouldn't have put her too out of reach to rub it in. Okay, God, I am listening; I am asking for help, direction, and guidance. I know I have your love, as you have mine as well. Thank you God for loving me, and I ask your help tonight in coming to the answers I have been begging to be answered. I also know that if I listen well, I will one day be rewarded, and I am thankful you selected me, yet another time and calling.

CHAPTER 3

About a month after my incident, Bishop Hein and I were walking through the market place getting some food items for the rectory, when I heard my name called out...

Father Thomas, Father Lance Thomas, good to see you out and about!

It was the rosary maker Tammy and her daughter Emily. Oh, what a joy to see their faces. She was at the market place selling some of her nicer rosaries, for some extra cash for their household. Her main place of work was her production company that she was still in the process of getting off the ground.

Tammy, always a pleasure to see you, Bishop Hein cut in, and was pleasant, even though I had not heard her call out <u>his</u> name. He was never a bitter man, and someone truly to admire.

Oh, Bishop Hein, would you like to bless this fine rosary this gentleman just purchased for his fiancé? I was hoping you would be stopping by...and I was just preparing to give him your contact information.

Tammy, this is one of your most beautiful rosaries yet. I would be delighted! His blessing included the upcoming marriage of the young couple, along with the rosary maker and her family in mind. The rosary was made of white freshwater pearls. *How beautiful are your rosaries today Tammy, always such fine quality!* He was quite the guy. He impressed me a great deal.

It bothered me that I was unable to bless the rosary for the young couple instead, however to step aside for a greater man was truly an honor, and to be acknowledged in his company was a greater one. Admiring all of the beautifully hand-crafted rosaries was a delight for any eye. She had quite the collection of Job's tears, glass marble beads, clay beads, plastic beads, and of course, the freshwater pearls in a variety of colors. The sunshine shown through most of them, and for those that it didn't; you could see the exquisite detail of each one. Her rosaries had circled the globe and back, with them traveling to Thailand, Africa, Poland, Germany, and of course, through-out the United States. Even crafters who weren't Catholic wanted one, and she gladly ordered and sold as many as she could that day. I was pleased with the work she had done, and I'm sure Our Lord was as well.

Before leaving, she gestured for me to come near, as I did; I noticed she was holding a small box. As I drew closer to her, she reached out and handed it to me. I thanked her, as I know she could see the surprised look on my face.

It's for your mother, her birthday... she trailed off.

Oh, my mother's birthday! Of course, how could I forget? (Recovering with a head injury, it was easier to forget more then I wanted to admit to myself.) My mother was a very loving, caring woman who would love all those around her. She was a quiet, gentle shorter woman who had all the strength a person could hold in their hearts. Her life was never an easy one, being raised with parents who didn't understand all that children needed to live a happy life, so she was adopted out into the family being raised by an Uncle and Aunt who had money, but they feared that Mother would take from them somehow, so she was cast as the outcast, born of outcast parents. After meeting Father, getting married, and having my sister and me, I know that she enjoyed each year she would spend with us as a family. She didn't deserve the suffering she endured, in life or with her cancer, but she didn't seem to mind. The day after her birthday, she passed in her sleep after her long journey with ovarian cancer. Father was already gone when she died, so it made things easier to think of the two of them together again. Every year, I had a tradition, on my mother's birthday, well for the past eight years anyway, after her death, of making it a point to come to the cemetery (no matter what I had going on) and placing a rosary for her, as I can remember years of praying the rosary together as a family. We would kneel on the floor as Father would lead the rosary, with Mother sitting by his side. We always prayed the rosary together. We understood that the family that prays together stays together; and that was correct in our case. After becoming a priest, she was so happy for me, and with me, that she visited the rectory so often, the other priests were thinking it odd that she was still 'mothering' me as she was; but I was the only boy in the family, I supposed it wasn't THAT odd that she would still treat me like that; it was easy to be singled out by mom, but only in a good way. As I thought about her, I continued staring at the box as if wondering what was inside. I decided that today was as good as any to go visit the small private cemetery in which she was laid to rest. I would put the radio on a good Christian-listening station, where they gladly quoted the bible and read from the testaments. I would enjoy getting out and about on my own today. The quiet drive to the country cemetery where she was buried would do me some good. Visiting would give me some normalcy in my life, and right now, I sure needed that. I missed Mother, as she was never really too far from my thoughts. I was wondering what she would think of what had happened to me. She probably would have suggested a rosary or a favorite song to listen to that would put our hearts into a happier, brighter place. Then, I believe she would have helped me move forward with my life.

My thoughts returned to reality, where I stood in the marketplace once again, in front of the booth where Tammy and her daughter were selling rosaries. Bishop Hein and I continued our walk around, stopping to visit with several vendors that we knew personally or were members of the parishes that we held mass in the past. I was glad that we had completed our walk in silence, as I was running out of things to say to these people who I barely remembered knowing. We smiled and made our presence known throughout the suburb in which we walked. It was a beautiful day, one that you see in pictures on the weather channel. Walking along, I looked up and tried to see animals and shapes in the clouds as my sister Lili and I used to do as children. We used to have so much fun with that on summer evenings, when there were so many colors in the sunset. Mother and Father would sit in their lawn chairs and tried desperately to see what it was that we were looking at.

After returning to the rectory, it was time for me to take that drive to the country. And I decided now was as good a time as any to go. I could still drive, and remembered how to very well; for some reason that part of my memory had not left me. I turned on the Christian radio station who was quoting Ecclesiastes. I knew the words they were saying were true, that there was a time and a place for everything under Heaven. Perhaps that time for me was now. As I came around the corner, I parked the rectory car at the front gate of the cemetery and got out with Tammy's rosary and box in my pocket. The cemetery was well kept. There were flowers and military flags that danced in the wind, as if to welcome me. Walking around the front of the car, I could see the shepherd's hook over her head stone. It was as beautiful as it was the day I bought it. I walked up to the headstone, reaching my destination. I knelt down and brushed the top of the stone clean from the fresh cut grass. The black marble stone looked back at me as though it was welcoming me. The sunshine helped me see my reflection as though I were looking into a mirror. The large white letters spelling out the last name THOMAS shone brightly in the day's sunshine. The engraved rosary on the front of the stone reminded me of the rosary in the box in my pocket, Tammy's box...that housed a homemade rosary, just for Mother. This year it was an etched emerald looking rosary with an Irish Celtic crucifix and center, just as Mother would have appreciated, as she was Irish, and very inspired by the view of a shamrock, as so many of her ancestors were during the time of Saint Patrick himself. I knelt down in honor of her.

Kneeling in prayer, blessing myself I prayed...

In the name of the Father, the Son, and the Holy Spirit. Amen.

I believe in God, the Father almighty, Creator of heaven and earth. I believe in Jesus Christ, his only Son, our Lord. He was conceived by the power of the Holy Spirit and born of the Virgin Mary. He suffered under Pontius Pilate, was crucified, died, and was buried. He ascended into heaven, and is seated at the right hand of the Father. He will come again to judge the living and the dead. I believe in the Holy Spirit, the holy Catholic Church, the communion of saints, the forgiveness of sins, the resurrection of the body, and life everlasting. Amen

For the increase of faith, hope, and charity...

Our Father who art in heaven, hallowed be Thy name; Thy Kingdom come; Thy will be done on earth as it is in heaven. Give us this day our daily bread; and forgive us our trespasses as we forgive those who trespass against us. And lead us not into temptation; but deliver us from evil. Amen

Hail Mary, full of grace, the Lord is with thee; blessed are you among women, and blessed is the fruit of your womb, Jesus. Holy Mary, Mother of God, pray for us sinners, now and at the hour of our death. Amen

Hail Mary, full of grace, the Lord is with thee; blessed are you among women, and blessed is the fruit of your womb, Jesus. Holy Mary, Mother of God, pray for us sinners, now and at the hour of our death. Amen

Hail Mary, full of grace, the Lord is with thee; blessed are you among women, and blessed is the fruit of your womb, Jesus. Holy Mary, Mother of God, pray for us sinners, now and at the hour of our death. Amen

Glory be to the Father, the Son, and the Holy Spirit, as it was in the beginning, is now, and ever shall be, world without end. Amen

Oh my Jesus, forgive us our sins, save us from the fires of hell; and lead all souls to heaven, especially those who are in most need of Thy mercy.

I continued to pray the rosary for the better part of an hour or so, wiping away tears in the process. Yes, tears. This priest knows how to pray, how to morn, and certainly how to feel and show feeling. Knowing she is in a better place didn't keep me from missing her. Especially around her birthday. I remember the gifts I had given her in the past, and as a child. I remember the magnet made from Popsicle sticks when I was in Grade school. That stayed on the fridge until I made her hide it when my friends would come over, and again on Prom night. Eventually it would show its age and break after falling on the floor. She cried into the night over that magnet, and now I realize she wasn't crying over the magnet itself, but what it represented, a younger, sweeter version of me that was no more. Well, eventually that sweeter version of me did find his way back home again, but as a man, not the little boy she once held in her arms.

Standing up, I pulled the blessed homemade rosary out of my hands that I had been praying upon, and I delicately hung it on the shepherd's hook. I hope she saw all of them glistening in the sunshine, from the eight years since she was gone. I was glad I had this moment with Mother today and was wondering to myself as I prayed if she might know God's plan for me. I wondered what she had hoped I had accomplished in my lifetime. She had never given her opinion, only support for what it was that we wanted to do with our lives. Perhaps, but just like all the gifts at Christmas time, some things she would feel would be worth keeping to one's self. With a large sigh, I walked away, glancing over my shoulder only once as I walked to the car.

CHAPTER 4

About a month went by, when my changes to my memory seemed obvious. I tried leading mass with Father Jameson, and hoped it would bring back some of what I had lost. I felt like a letdown to those who noticed that I was reading notes written on post-its in the liturgy book, the hymnal, and even reading my written homily, which was written by Bishop Hein, with me in mind. I was beginning to feel as though I was losing everything. I remembered the joys of being a priest and I wanted to remain being a priest, however some things were no longer coming easy for me, and I began to wonder why this part of my life is one that must go. It's all I know, really. Other than my sister and her family, I had no one in the world, with both Mother and Father gone. My memories of them remained to keep me company during the daytime hours, but there was the stillness of the night I had a difficult time getting through. I wondered how I would manage to fill my days with all that I had before me gone. It left uncertainty in my thoughts. However, I admit that thinking of my parents made me feel better, almost as good as if they were right here with me.

My father was a glider pilot in World War II, very young, but good at his post. I heard many stories of bravery from himself as well as from the few that came home alive with him. He was a very hard worker, even working two jobs at one time, as money was tight when my sister was a baby, I remember. My mother didn't meet Father until the end of the war, but it was one of those romances that you read about in novels, from what I heard. Their courtship lasted two weeks, before getting married in a borrowed white dress and an army uniform. The honeymoon lasted as long as I knew them. They were always winking at each other, stealing kisses when we weren't in the room, and reminding each other how lucky they were for the other one. It was cute until we grew up and understood it better. I remember thinking it was very unpleasant at the time, however now looking back and remembering them; I find it almost refreshing. How much easier all marriages would be if everyone were that loving to their spouse, and as kind with their words and actions.

Later that day, I found myself in prayer, praying for all marriages, not only those that I have united in the sacrament of marriage, but those that really needed saving... I also found myself reading my prayers off of a cheat-sheet, but prayers I was still praying; for all those in need and for me, for direction and guidance.

The First Joyful Mystery, the Annunciation...

Our Father who art in heaven, hallowed be Thy name; Thy Kingdom come; Thy will be done on earth as it is in heaven. Give us this day our daily bread; and forgive us our trespasses as we forgive those who trespass against us. And lead us not into temptation; but deliver us from evil. Amen.

Hail Mary, full of grace, the Lord is with thee; blessed are you among women, and blessed is the fruit of your womb, Jesus. Holy Mary, Mother of God, pray for us sinners, now and at the hour of our death. Amen

Hail Mary, full of grace, the Lord is with thee; blessed are you among women, and blessed is the fruit of your womb, Jesus. Holy Mary, Mother of God, pray for us sinners, now and at the hour of our death. Amen

Hail Mary, full of grace, the Lord is with thee; blessed are you among women, and blessed is the fruit of your womb, Jesus. Holy Mary, Mother of God, pray for us sinners, now and at the hour of our death. Amen....

As difficult as it was to read my prayers off of the sheet, I had to admit to myself that the more I prayed them, the more I remembered them. Perhaps this was a break-through of my condition. I looked forward to my next doctor visit, which was later today. I was so thrilled to be able to add something to the visit, instead of having to listen to the doctor explain how things were only going to be getting worse. This was a break-through, I was sure of it. I was determined to come out ahead of all of this. It was the new and improved me - and I was ready to embrace it!

As Bishop Hein drove me to the doctor's office later that day, I know I had a smile on my face, as he asked me why.

Why do you think? I asked him matter-of-factly. *I* **remember** *something, that is getting better, and I am happy to say that my days of leading mass from notes may be in the near future, and praying from cheat-sheets will soon be done with as well, as I will soon have everything memorized again, and I will be back at mass, as a priest! I know you would appreciate seeing me behind the altar, and I would deeply appreciate it too.*

I was so thrilled to be able to exclaim to him my small steps of recovery. My excitement faded when we were in the doctor's office. It hurt to hear what the doctor had to say...

There will be times when you may feel as though you have reached the end of this and are making a comeback, and that may be; however we need to check more than just that part of your memory. There are such vast differences in the sections of the brain that were injured. In fact, further tests have now shown us that you had two injuries; one from the lightening, and one from falling on the sidewalk. Two different sections of the brain to look at now, and no idea when this will end or if your memory will ever recover. Sometimes patients remember by re-memorizing facts from their past, then somehow are able to remember from that. Often time, you could find that it's the smallest things that can jog your memory, such as a vision or a certain sound. Studies have shown that its often times both of those combined. Today's scan will be evaluated for further damage, and we will give you a call to notify you of any new developments. Now do you have any questions?

I sat there numb. No idea what to say. It hurt to hear him say those words to me. I don't remember responding to his question, I only remember leaving the doctor's office after that.

All I knew to do at this point was pray, and I prayed on the way back to the rectory...

Hail Mary, full of grace, the Lord is with thee; blessed are you among women, and blessed is the fruit of your womb, Jesus. Holy Mary, Mother of God, pray for us sinners, now and at the hour of our death. Amen....

Hail Mary, full of grace, the Lord is with thee; blessed are you among women, and blessed is the fruit of your womb, Jesus. Holy Mary, Mother of God, pray for us sinners, now and at the hour of our death. Amen....

Bishop Hein broke my prayers at that point as he spoke to me.

How about you and I stop to visit the orphans at the group home before going back to the rectory. Maybe it will do you some good.

I agree; my response was quick. Going back to the rectory only reminded me of what I didn't know, what I couldn't remember, and what I wished I'd had.

We pulled up in front of the Sacred Heart Home for Orphans. It was a larger home on a corner lot. The siding was a bright white with a front porch that wrapped half way around the front of the house. The corner rooms were rounded as if it were a castle, giving it a fairytale charm. The woman who met us at the door was an older lady named Mary Kilby. She was very pleasant as she welcomed us in. She asked us if there was anything that we wanted to drink or eat, as she just had baked cookies and made a pitcher of ice tea. She was very cordial. I thought of how this wonderful person was the perfect choice to be in charge of an Orphanage.

Upon entering the orphanage, I noticed a small young boy in the corner with a big pout on his face. It had looked as though he was in some kind of trouble. It took me back to my own days of time-outs and being in trouble. I could remember the time I had a toad in a pail in the basement. I would catch insects all day just to keep that toad in the pail. I was getting good at catching flies, shaking them in my hand, and putting them in that pail with the toad, while they were still twitching. It was a great concept until Mother had figured out what I was up to. It wasn't long before she paid attention to my whereabouts and found the toad. It broke my heart to let that toad go out in the garden. But Mother said it was time it found its own food. The worst part was my protesting to the point where I found myself looking at the corner for a while. Mother wasn't unreasonable, unless I was first; and when it came to my toad, I was quite defensive. I learned my lesson that day... always be on the lookout for someone following you, as it might be a person who wants to put you on a time-out! I had a difficult time just standing there.

A smile came over my face when I recalled those young childhood moments, and I prayed silently in my heart that those memories would never go away. Upon looking around the orphanage, I remembered being at this place, although my memories were clouded somehow. As if able to read my mind, or what I was thinking, Bishop Hein spoke to me while in thought.

Let's take a walk down this hallway, Bishop Hein insisted; *maybe it will jog a memory or two for you.*

Something about this place I remember, I shared, *but nothing that would do anyone much good.*

Don't be so sure of it Father Thomas, he was smiling now bigger than ever.

I couldn't figure out what the big deal was all of a sudden. Did he notice that I had been daydreaming and remembering my own childhood? Perhaps that's all it was. We were slowing down near the main fork in the hallway where I noticed the donor's information on the wall. There was a plaque that read "This house donated by Mrs. Margaret Thomas as a home for orphans".

Mother! I remembered. *This was my childhood home! That explains the memories that I started to remember upon entering this home!*

Above the plaque was our family picture. It was a picture of my sister Lili in a wagon, with me, the big brother stood holding the handle. Mother and Father were standing behind us with their arms around one another. It was a picture worth cherishing, and something to remember! I know why remembering came so easy. It all makes sense again. I took the picture off the wall and held it close to my chest, as if to hug it. I was so happy that tears came to my eyes, and they began to fall. I stood there in the hallway crying, clutching my past with great triumph! It didn't take me long to realize that I was the only one in the hallway. Bishop Hein had decided to leave me be, and went to visit with

Mary, and to take care of the children. Before putting the picture back on the wall, I had noticed there was a hand-written note on the back of the picture, written in ink.

It read:

Do what you want to upkeep the house, but do not move the pail in the basement.

Thank you & God Bless!

Margaret Thomas

I quickly hung the picture on the wall, and hurried to the basement steps. I flung open the door and shuffled my way down the steps. No one was allowed to play down here, so things looked the way they had when I was a kid. I found the pail in the "hiding" place in the basement where I had kept the toad. The original pail was still sitting there. It was such a step back in time that I was almost expecting there to be a toad in the pail when I got there. Instead what I found was a folded up piece of paper.

It read:

Dearest Lance and Lili,

If you are reading this, you have come here looking for answers of some kind. I am not going to be around to console you when this happens, but please know that I am with you always, so your answers will need to come from within. You have always been led by your heart, so if you are questioning things, let your heart guide you. Remember, you can always come home, but you can never go back. I love you more than all the insects in the garden.

Love, Mother

Her words brought out more tears. I don't remember missing her as much as I did right now. The emotions that flooded over me were so strong; I didn't know how I would handle things. I stood there, holding the note in Mother's handwriting, looking at the pail and remembering days gone by. I prayed that the memories that I was remembering would stay with me. It hurt that I felt like I was losing the best part of me. Perhaps I just needed some remodeling of my own. Always room for improvement, perhaps. I folded the note and put it back into the pail. I soon realized that I wasn't alone. The young boy from the corner was hiding out in the basement with me. He wasn't supposed to be down here, so I quickly inquired.

Are you supposed to be down here? I asked him.

NO! Was the answer.

What are you doing down here?

I got sumthin' back there. He pointed over to the opposite corner.

I walked over and discovered that there was a toad sitting on a brick. He looked like the toad I used to have!

I said to him, *This looks just like the toad I used to have as a kid!*

Really? Cool!

Do you feed it insects? I inquired further.

Not since I got in trubbl' with Miss Mary. Now we just talk.

I was really curious...*What does he say?*

Nuttin', cause it's a toad. Toads don't talk.

Of course toads don't talk. I knew that. Do you talk to the toad? They like that.

Yep. We're good friends. Talk ever' day.

Good and glad to hear it! Mine liked it when I talked to him too. Keeps them healthy. What do you say we go upstairs and get some lunch? I bet you're hungry.

Without hesitation, we went upstairs as it was time to get washed up for lunch. It put a smile on my face thinking that this toad was probably a relative of the toad that I once kept in my pail as a kid. It gave me happy warm fuzzies. Knowing that somehow the toad family was still in the basement, that thought alone made me want to visit the orphanage more often. Perhaps I would make it a point to do so, and talk to the young lad who liked talking to his toad, as I had once enjoyed talking to mine.

Chapter 5

Days later, I was in prayer at the rectory.

Hail Mary, full of grace, the Lord is with thee; blessed are you among women, and blessed is the fruit of your womb, Jesus. Holy Mary, Mother of God, pray for us sinners, now and at the hour of our death. Amen.

Hail Mary, full of grace, the Lord is with thee; blessed are you among women, and blessed is the fruit of your womb, Jesus. Holy Mary, Mother of God, pray for us sinners, now and at the hour of our death. Amen.

Hail Mary, full of grace, the Lord is with thee; blessed are you among women, and blessed is the fruit of your womb, Jesus. Holy Mary, Mother of God, pray for us sinners, now and at the hour of our death. Amen.

Hail Mary, full of grace, the Lord is with thee; blessed are you among women, and blessed is the fruit of your womb, Jesus. Holy Mary, Mother of God, pray for us sinners, now and at the hour of our death. Amen.

Hail Mary, full of grace, the Lord is with thee; blessed are you among women, and blessed is the fruit of your womb, Jesus. Holy Mary, Mother of God, pray for us sinners, now and at the hour of our death. Amen.

Glory be to the Father, the Son, and the Holy Spirit, as it was in the beginning, is now, and ever shall be, world without end. Amen

Oh my Jesus, forgive us our sins, save us from the fires of hell; and lead all souls to heaven, especially those who are in most need of Thy mercy.

My cell phone rang. It was the Sacred Heart Home for Orphans.

Hello Miss Mary, and how may I help you?

Father Thomas, I have a concern. She sounded concerned! *The young man Koalton, whom you talked to in the basement the other day has fallen ill, and he's asking for you. I have an adoption agency coming over today, and I must be here to see them, so I can't go with him. I was wondering if you would be kind enough to go with him to see the doctor.*

Yes! I would be happy to. What time would you like me to pick him up?

As soon as you can get here, Father; he's not well.

I rushed to the main room of the rectory, where I noticed Bishop Hein reading today's paper.

Busy? I asked.

Need to go somewhere? He inquired.

One of the kids are sick. Miss Mary just called.

Grabbing his paper to read in the waiting room, we both left with rosaries in our pockets.

We arrived at the clinic with Koalton, his insurance information, and symptoms that were difficult to understand. I knew nothing of his background, so if there was a problem in his genetics, it would be unknown to us all. Bishop Hein filled out the information on the form as we waited in the waiting room. I glanced around to all those that were waiting with us that day. Some were coughing, some were sneezing, some were walking around on crutches, and some were waiting with someone else, all kinds of people from all walks of life. I glanced around and wondered what brought each and every one of these people to this place. Just then I heard…

Father Thomas!

Looking over, I noticed Tammy was there with her daughter.

Tammy, what a pleasant surprise, what brings you here? I asked her, noticing that her daughter had a tissue in her hand.

Well, it seems like seasonal allergies again, but it's best to make sure. How about you Father…another doctor visit perhaps?

Nope, just hanging out with Bishop Hein and Koalton. Not sure what to expect, so we await the doctors decision, when he gets a chance to see us. I kept conversation light today. No need to frighten the children, after all.

Just then the nurse opened the door. She called out a name...

Emily

Gotta go Father! The nurse called out Tammy's daughter's name. And they disappeared behind the door, as they followed the nurse. Shortly thereafter, they called Koalton's name, and we went in the same door.

After testing, it was discovered that Koalton had received a mild poisoning from the toad. He either didn't wash his hands properly, or he licked the frog or kissed it on the head, not sure which. He didn't remember either, so I was glad I wasn't the only one not remembering things. After a long lecture from the doctor about properly handing the toad, we received a box of rubber gloves, medicine and were off for the day, stopping off for an ice cream treat at the corner ice cream stand on the way back to Sacred Heart Home for Orphans.

Weeks past and I reached the point of frustration, as I could no longer consecrate hosts into the body, or wine into blood. My parish was accepting of Father Jameson, and I thought he did rather well, for someone with little or no experience. I thought it best to accept what I at first refused to accept; to retire as a priest, or step-down completely if the Diocese refused my reasoning. I sat down at my desk and I conducted myself with as much priestly honesty as I could, as I wrote the letter that would change my life forever...

Your Excellency, Bishop Hein,

I would like your permission to resign from my position as a priest.

I have not had my memory come to full recovery and I am more and more discouraged as I find myself remembering less and less.

Please accept the fact that I can no longer perform my priestly duties and feel it necessary to take this route. I am open to your suggestions.

Yours in Christ, Father Lance Thomas

I swallowed hard as I re-read the simple words on paper. I don't know what bothered me more, not knowing who or what I was; or my uncertain future. I told myself that it was a little of both. I placed the letter in a manila envelope as I knew not to fold it, for documentation purposes. I put the envelope on my desk, as I prepared myself to give it to him. I decided to go in prayer.

The Second Joyful Mysteries, The Visitation...

Our Father who art in heaven, hallowed be Thy name; Thy Kingdom come; Thy will be done on earth as it is in heaven. Give us this day our daily bread; and forgive us our trespasses as we forgive those who trespass against us. And lead us not into temptation; but deliver us from evil. Amen.

Hail Mary, full of grace, the Lord is with thee; blessed are you among women, and blessed is the fruit of your womb, Jesus. Holy Mary, Mother of God, pray for us sinners, now and at the hour of our death. Amen

Hail Mary, full of grace, the Lord is with thee; blessed are you among women, and blessed is the fruit of your womb, Jesus. Holy Mary, Mother of God, pray for us sinners, now and at the hour of our death. Amen

Hail Mary, full of grace, the Lord is with thee; blessed are you among women, and blessed is the fruit of your womb, Jesus. Holy Mary, Mother of God, pray for us sinners, now and at the hour of our death. Amen

Hail Mary, full of grace, the Lord is with thee; blessed are you among women, and blessed is the fruit of your womb, Jesus. Holy Mary, Mother of God, pray for us sinners, now and at the hour of our death. Amen

Hail Mary, full of grace, the Lord is with thee; blessed are you among women, and blessed is the fruit of your womb, Jesus. Holy Mary, Mother of God, pray for us sinners, now and at the hour of our death. Amen

Mary Buford

You look like you're really in thought Father Thomas. Bishop Hein's voice startled me, as I thought I was alone in prayer. He continued, *I didn't mean to startle you, however I was wondering how you were coming along...the memory, and your own doctor visits..?*

I looked up from my rosary, and was silent. I had nothing to say to him at that time, so I just handed him the envelope, and went on praying...or tried to. He opened the envelope and said nothing, either. I guess there is an odd silence that goes on and on between two people sometimes. I wish I knew now what that was called, however, that long silence is what took place between us that day, and let down was felt. He broke the silence...

You are welcome to stay here with us as long as you like, as your childhood home was given to the church, I think it only fair that the church allow you to stay. Also, I pray that it brings back some of your memory, as I am in high hopes of your religious return. You are a wonderful priest, and I think I'll wait before turning this into the Diocese. I want to make sure you are comfortable with your decision first. I also see that you would appreciate some prayer time. Enjoy your day, Father Thomas!

With that said, he left the room, and left me in prayer once more.

CHAPTER 6

Today was a different one for me. I decided that since I was going to resign as a priest, I took off my white roman collar. I know those who all noticed, or didn't notice, even though no one said anything to me directly.

I decided to go out and take a walk, and find myself in the real world. God would always be with me, and I knew he loved me, but now I had to rediscover myself.

Who was I?

What did I like to do before the seminary?

Was I interested in the arts? Played any sports? Sang? Danced? Played an instrument?

I guess in my new self-discovery, I needed to learn who I was once again. I felt as though I had lost my identity, but yet I knew who I was; however most of what I had done in my life was gone. Should I look at the priesthood as a profession, in other words someone in search of a new job? I had no answers, only my athletic shoes, my jeans, and my grey Catholic Youth Rally tee-shirt. I guess I thought I was just some guy walking along blending in, when I heard a familiar voice call out my name...

Father Thomas! Nice to see you! It was Father Jameson from my former parish. *Mind if I walk with you a while? I'm on my way to get a new batch of rosaries!*

Don't mind if you do Father! Calling him Father was humorous to me, as he seemed more like a son than anything. *I was thinking of walking that direction myself.*

Why I said that, I'll never know. I had no intention of visiting Tammy today, even though she had crossed my mind a few times. The thing was, she still spoke to me gently and kindly, and without hesitation. Most of the parishioners stopped talking to me, for fear of who I was or had become. I didn't understand why, but they seemed to have their reasons individually. It hurt me to see parents re-directing their children away from me the one Sunday, as I sat in the pews among them. I prayed for them, and still continued to, for as long as I could.

When we arrived at Tammy & Emily's residence, we discovered they were praying the rosary as they did every day...

Hail Mary, full of grace, the Lord is with thee; blessed are you among women, and blessed is the fruit of your womb, Jesus. Holy Mary, Mother of God, pray for us sinners, now and at the hour of our death. Amen

Hail Mary, full of grace, the Lord is with thee; blessed are you among women, and blessed is the fruit of your womb, Jesus. Holy Mary, Mother of God, pray for us sinners, now and at the hour of our death. Amen

Hail Mary, full of grace, the Lord is with thee; blessed are you among women, and blessed is the fruit of your womb, Jesus. Holy Mary, Mother of God, pray for us sinners, now and at the hour of our death. Amen

Hail Mary, full of grace, the Lord is with thee; blessed are you among women, and blessed is the fruit of your womb, Jesus. Holy Mary, Mother of God, pray for us sinners, now and at the hour of our death. Amen

Hail Mary, full of grace, the Lord is with thee; blessed are you among women, and blessed is the fruit of your womb, Jesus. Holy Mary, Mother of God, pray for us sinners, now and at the hour of our death. Amen

Glory be to the Father, the Son, and the Holy Spirit, as it was in the beginning, is now, and ever shall be, world without end. Amen

Oh my Jesus, forgive us our sins, save us from the fires of hell; and lead all souls to heaven, especially those who are in most need of Thy mercy.

Father Jameson and Father Thomas, what a wonderful surprise! She was happy to see us both. She always had that way with her. *Father Jameson, your rosaries - about a dozen, if that's okay for now.*

Yes-Of course Tammy! I love getting your rosaries! How blessed a woman who makes rosaries for her priests! Wow, I was thinking to myself, that was grateful indeed, but a bit over the top from how I act toward her. I suppose a person so pleasant; it's easy to be pleasant back.

Would either of you like a slice of lemon meringue pie? My Grandmother's recipe...

Well how many guys do you know who would turn down a piece of pie!? I remarked.

I must, I'm afraid, Father Jameson declined. *Health reasons are my only excuse.*

Well, Father Thomas, how about you?

Of course, lemon meringue pie! That sounds like great!

Would you like to visit a while, or would you like to take it with you? She seemed hopeful that we would stay.

I have to be getting back Tammy; however Father Thomas is more that welcome to have a bite with you.

I'll stay Tammy, I said to her, *no reason to visit and run for me.*

Even though I had no idea why I was visiting today, but something just seemed to feel right. I guess I needed somewhere to go. Her home is a pleasant one, and adorned with religious artifacts. She has a large wall rosary blessed by me that came from Bethlehem. She has pictures of the saints, several crucifixes and crosses - one in each room of the house (yes even the bathroom!), and holy water fonts through-out. She has several pictures of her daughter Emily, which all but takes up any remaining wall space. She is a simple person with religious tastes. It's easy to visit her home, and feel comfortable.

The pie was one of the best that I ever tasted, or so I remembered. She knew how to bake up this stuff with her Grandmother's recipes. As mentioned, she was a heavy-set person, but it looked good on her. She wasn't odd proportioned, nor did she dress like a slob. She was herself, and that's what looked best on her. Above her stove I noticed a sign that read:

"DON'T TAKE FOOD ADVICE FROM A THIN WOMAN!"

I guess that would describe her well. Someone who probably wouldn't take advice from anyone anyway, but certainly a reminder that thin women might not know about food. Either way, it was comical! I know what it meant, and it described her well.

We talked the better part of the afternoon, and I confided in her how I felt about the church, the confusion, and the priesthood. I felt as though I could tell her anything, as she was one of my parishioners that I confided in often, or at least what I remember. Even though I knew that I shouldn't tell everything to her, I did. I was expecting not to regret it. Before leaving, I walked to the door, and she asked me to wait, as she was going to send a piece of pie home with me. I gladly accepted and waited a moment longer, and soon she would return with the pie in a to-go container. As I prepared to open the door and leave, I swung around and gave her a hug. Big mistake.

The moment my arms were around her, I wished I didn't have to let go. I breathed in her fragrance, felt her hair on my cheek, and pressing against her warmth made me think of nothing else but her. Even though she did nothing more than return the hug, it was in her arms that I wanted to be, now and forever. How odd, I felt; as I thought about being a disappointment to the church, and getting down on myself for not able to perform priestly duties, to wanting to be in her arms until the end of time. How could all that change with just one hug? That's some hug! All those emotions going through me in one day! How could I tell that to her and betray her trust? I was so concerned that she wouldn't understand all the feelings and emotions that I was feeling at this moment. Everything inside me said to tell her, or ask to stay longer. Holding her in my arms was one of the most incredible moments of my life. Never have I had the same feeling in my fingertips as in my toes, or the pounding pulse in my ears while I could hear every breath that she made when I held her for that brief moment. The flood of emotions almost over took me as I felt something, I felt her emotions as well as my own, but most importantly above all other things, and I felt as though I were home.

After leaving Tammy's home, I couldn't help but try to get my thoughts and emotions in check. After all, I had been a priest for 15 years, in addition to the time I studied in the seminary. Even though I was awaiting to hear if I could walk away from the priesthood, how would I explain this to Tammy, or even her daughter Emily; whom I have had serve my masses so many times before. I had no idea what I was thinking, or my thoughts, nor did I want to try to explain my thoughts to anyone at this point. It just seemed right to hold her; and it was just a hug as far as I was concerned, so perhaps I should just keep my thoughts to myself. Perhaps it would be better that way. I decided it was time to thinking about it as not to confuse myself.

I returned to the rectory with enough time to place my pie (my little slice of heaven - so to speak) in my room, as I felt as though it was my little treasure from home. I was surprised that there wasn't anyone around, no one. I looked at the calendar and wondered if there was something going on that I had missed somehow. I needed to start writing more things down, but what is important, and what isn't. I'm guessing that I missed something important. Soon, my thoughts were interrupted by talking and laughter from outside as the priests were returning. I chose to avoid them by going to my room. I still had thoughts of Tammy and her hug from earlier, and wondered if she was having the same thoughts that I was. It would be tricky to ask her, and I felt as though it would be best to just leave it alone. How could I avoid how I felt or how I was thinking. Since the lightning strike, all everyone kept asking was how was I thinking, remembering, or my thought process behind any given thought at the moment. How could I deny having these thoughts? It wasn't right for a priest to think these thoughts, certainly no; but a man who doesn't remember how to be a priest, and who is lost in this world certainly would find comfort in someone's arms, especially someone as kind, generous, and loving as Tammy. How could any man deny knowing her or knowing what her needs were, and most importantly, why would he want to?

I found myself thinking of her that night as I drifted off to sleep, into a dream...

{*I was standing on shore on a dock of some sort, in the fog. No idea of a body of water, maybe a lake, maybe a stream; not for certain. The fog was heavy, like a dense rain-forest view from the sky. I was just standing there, in dress clothes. I was waiting for something or someone; I didn't know who or what, but I was waiting. No one was with me, just me. Off in the distance I saw a small row boat. I couldn't tell if it was coming towards me or if it was going away from me, as the fog was so dense I could barely see. I was so interested in the small boat that seemed to be so close, yet so far away. I heard something behind me, so I turned around. In the midst of the fog was a male lion. His mane was long, and it flowed in the breeze; the color of the mane was a deep golden color, it almost looked like it was on fire. On his head was a crown made of the brightest gold with two initials etched in the gold...A, the alpha, and Ω, the omega. There were three stones on the crown. Taking a second look, I realized that the three stones represented the holy trilogy: God the Father, God the Son, and God the Holy Spirit.The middle stone was larger than the other two, and a very bright white diamond. The stone on the left was a fire & ice stone, a clear crystal that had a burst of red bled through half of it. The third stone was a deep sapphire marbled with clear white crystal. The lion stood still looking at me, directly in my eyes. I looked back at him, in his eyes. He didn't attack me nor did he run from me, he just looked at me, in a calm-seeming way. Just then a small bird flew in our view of each other, and with that, the lion was gone. The small bird, a sparrow, perched itself on the dock pole near where I was standing. It was hurt. I could see blood splatter on one of its wings. Its wing was broken. I reached out to help it, but it looked at me as if it were scared. Of course a bird wouldn't have the bravery of a lion. I pulled back, waiting once again. I heard a voice behind me say "Lance, do you have what it takes to heal all her wounds?" When I turned back around, it was the lion again. [Did the lion just speak to me? I asked this question to myself over and over.] Again, when I looked at the bird, I heard the question again "Lance, do you have what it takes to heal all her wounds?" "YES!" I answered the voice, now not sure if it came from the bird or the lion. I hurried my glance behind me, to find the lion gone, then turning back, forward facing, so was the sparrow. The fog was starting to lift, and I could finally see the row boat out on the water, a silhouette at first, then more clearly. It wasn't going toward me or away, it was tied to the dock. Reaching down to grab the rope, I noticed that the threads were golden colored, similar to the lion's mane. I started to pull the rope towards shore, and found the boat moving with it, toward me now. In the boat sat someone. Was this where the voice came from? Who was in the boat? I pulled and pulled with all my might, until I noticed the person in the boat was Tammy! There she was afloat all along, and here I was, so close, yet so far away. I was able to help her come to shore. Was she so lost that I would need to pull her toward me? Was SHE who the voice kept asking about when it asked the question regarding "having what it takes to heal all HER wounds"?}*

I awoke. Glancing at my clock, it was 15 minutes before it would wake me for church. Startled by the dream, I was laying back and thinking many thoughts. I looked forward to talking to Tammy. Her thoughts and actions (the hug) may have sparked something inside me that was truly a once in a lifetime moment. Seeing her again, I wanted to tell her everything, from how I felt, to how she might feel. I wasn't sure what to say. In addition to her, clearly I needed to speak with Bishop Hein, as it's possible that he would look at the dream as nothing to be so concerned over. I didn't know how to talk to him about this, after knowing how he felt about my resigning. I took a deep breath, and let it out slowly, before getting up to start the day. I knelt on the side of my bed to pray.

Lord, please continue to guide me in what it is you are asking of me. I ask to be your guided vessel on the sea. Please show me my purpose, and I will do your will. I ask this in Jesus' name. Amen.

I decided to go on-line and look up the meanings of dreams, starting with the broken wing bird, possibly a sparrow. On line research took me to various places. It was obvious about the lion. I felt as if it was the Almighty coming to me in my dream, making sure I was ready for the changes that he was doing to me, or I may have been doing to myself, as well. The part of the dream that baffled me the most was the bird. What does a bird with a broken wing mean? I referenced until I found a few plausible answers. They ranged anywhere from feeling weak, to being a healer. I was both, in one sense or another. I looked into the possibility that I was going to make all her hurts go away. (Lord, I hope so.) I wanted to make mine go away as well, although now that didn't seem all that important to me. I looked further and found that the drifting boat had a lot to do with memory. The parts that I remembered, and the parts that I didn't remember were calling out to me. There was something special about Tammy being in the boat. I wasn't quite sure what the boat meant, until I continued to read on and found the answer that I was looking for. The water represented a natural element, such as a natural disaster. The drifting was about my emotions. Tammy was in the boat that was drifting. Tammy was all about my emotions. It was about her after all. Was this my mind, or my heart, or God telling me this? I was beginning to wonder. I was hoping to have more dreams to guide me through this difficult time in my life. Perhaps these dreams were like treasure maps to the way and the truth of my life, and its purpose.

CHAPTER 7

Church was hardly filled when I arrived, as it was very early this morning, yet. I wanted to catch Bishop Hein and see what his plans were for the rest of the day. I found him in the confessional alone, so I decided to join him for a moment. We set a time that worked well for us, after lunch to meet at the tennis courts. Apparently I used to like to play tennis. Well, it would be good exercise and good for a laugh as well. It would be interesting to see how well I would play a sport I used to remember how to play, keyword being 'remembered'.

Mass went as planned, then home for a quick bite, prayer, then meet Bishop Hein and off to the tennis courts. The day was a rather sunny day, not many clouds in the sky; the kind of day I didn't mind being out in. We hit the tennis ball back and forth for a while before he asked what was going on. I started to tell a little bit about the dream that I had, I hardly said anything, when he drew in a breath and began...

I don't know if you decided to share this with me because you need answers, or if you are looking for spiritual direction; however I don't have anything to tell you, that would help you, I'm afraid. Father Lance Thomas was a priest, YOU were a priest, that I could count on to do most/any-thing I ask of him. You are questioning all things, and I'm sorry, however I am not used to the new YOU yet. As to your dream, you should follow your heart, as I don't know what else you can do to bring this all back to you. You could study all over again and regain your priesthood if that's an option; but I fear that your heart and mind are made up, and don't know if I can persuade you into NOT trying out new avenues. Being alone is not all that it's cracked up to be, I know from personal experience; and now you are asking me to help assist you in what could change the views of most in the congregation. Lance, honestly, I understand being confused, if this is what it is; however make sure so you don't end up hurting others, as well as yourself, because I guarantee that the Diocese will not take your memory loss into account if they need to punish you. I am asking and telling you at this point, please don't do anything you will regret later.

He didn't say anything the rest of the tennis practice, nor did he say anything on the drive back to the rectory. I was taken back, so to speak. I thought that this was something he might know something about. Bishop Hein seemed frustrated and upset by my constant companionship. Going to see him was top of my list originally, but that was turning out to be not the best decision I made. Perhaps he could have suggested what the talking lion signified or the bird with the broken wing. Maybe I needed to talk to Tammy and get her views on this. I would call her upon our arrival back to the rectory.

Or so I thought. Cardinal Jefferson was waiting for me in the dining room of the rectory when we arrived. He called me to sit down. His face was blank, and I found this expression extremely difficult to read.

We received your paperwork on leaving the priesthood. I have to say that I am not pleased; however given your current condition, I am afraid there is little to do to stop you. There is a suggested course of action to take to make it official, I would seriously consider doing just that. Of course, you are welcome to remain here at the rectory, granted that your actions remain just and you maintain your vow of celibacy. Am I clear Father Thomas? He was sharp.

Yes Cardinal Jefferson, I understand, and realize that I need to conduct myself appropriately.

I am leaving you the necessary paperwork to fill out so we can further clear your vows. It's a shame Father; I understand you were quite the priest. Please continue to be in contact with us and keep us well informed as we don't wish for you to be conducting yourself in a way that would question the faith of others in this profession. Good afternoon Father.

With that he was off, and I was still sitting there. I was not sure how to take the "mouthful" I was just handed, however I was now well informed. With these thoughts going around and round in my head I decided to take a walk. Stepping outside I thought about talking to Tammy, but somehow felt as though she might receive the news as badly as Bishop Hein. I did not want to risk that, as how she felt would make me walk on water, or sink into the bottoms. I felt as though seeing her right now might make me even more vulnerable, something that I did not need.

I decided to take a walk around the park, instead. It wouldn't be too crowded, but still have the joyous laughter of children running and playing, with their parents close by. Couples would be out walking hand-in-hand while whispers of promises on their lips. I could see the slightest hint of the sunset as the late afternoon sun was still higher in the sky. I was in a relaxed state when I heard my name..

Father Thomas! It was Tammy once again. It's funny how everywhere I went she seemed to be.

Hello Tammy, my FAVORITE rosary maker; what a pleasant surprise!

Father, you were looking like you were in deep thought; I almost didn't say anything. How are you? How are things at the rectory?

Oh fine, fine; you know. I tried to keep conversation light and airy this evening. [*Tell her, tell her!]* I was thinking to myself. I wanted to tell her, but how?

Father, would you like to go back to my place for a cup of hot cocoa, or a glass of warm milk? That always seems to keep things calm with me.

I should have declined, however I wanted to go, I mean, I really wanted to go with HER!

Yes, I'd love to. Hot cocoa, watching the sun go down... Who could ask for anything more? I guess I was trying to be upbeat, but came across sounding really eager, too eager!

We walked to her place, and along the way we shared some small talk, but nothing I would really call a conversation. The forecast called for a cooler breeze, maybe a shower or two, but nothing too serious to worry too much about. The walk was a longer one, and I had my mind on talking with her about what was going on in my head, and my heart. I really wanted to learn to be a priest again, as I knew at one time I enjoyed it, not that I could remember much, if any of it. Having someone to share my life with was important to me at this point of my life, and having that companionship would out-weigh all other important factors in my mind.

We reached Tammy's place and went inside. Her daughter had stayed home studying for a test the next day, and she almost greeted us at the door as she was taking a break from her studies.

Hello Father Thomas! It's nice that you walked Mom home. In a few moments I will need to get back to studying. I have plenty to study, so I hope you don't think I'm ignoring you, but I have this test tomorrow, and it's a good share of my grade for the semester!

Oh, Emily I know how hard you were studying and don't have any intentions to disturb you. I understand how important getting good grades are. Good luck tomorrow. Your mother and I were just going to visit for a while. I guess she went off to the kitchen to make some hot cocoa, shall I ask her to count you in for that?

No thanks, it'll keep me up late. You go ahead.

I smiled at Emily as I walked into the kitchen where Tammy had disappeared to. She had the cocoa/dried milk mixture out that I remembered having at her place before. [How was it that I could remember that and not other things that were somewhat or more important?] This memory thing was like learning steps to a dance. I remember some of the steps, but the overall outcome was nothing like it should be, I thought to myself as I noticed she was trying to get my attention.

Marshmallows like usual?

I was almost startled.

Yes please, always the marshmallows and you don't have to ask me twice!

I was like a kid when it came to sweets, the more the merrier. We sat across from one another at her kitchen table that evening, and I was beginning to wonder what she would think of what I wanted to tell her, since she and her daughter were still addressing me as "Father". I wanted to tell her how I was no longer going to be a priest for too much longer, and I wanted to tell her how her hug the other day really made me feel; but it all stopped when I saw her take a drink of her hot cocoa. I watched her. I watched her every move. If women were my new vice, then she was the lock and key. She raised her hot cocoa mug to her lips and blew on it gently so she didn't burn herself. She must have realized she just took it off the stove, so she blew on it a few more times before taking a sip. I noticed the way her lips curled inward when she drew in her first sip. I noticed she was wearing some sort of lip gloss that day, and throughout the day, most had worn off. I was noticing her breaths she took as she drew in another sip. She was placing her mug down, and with just a hint of melted marshmallow on her lips, I saw them move. The structure of the forming of her lips caused me to notice her more and more, and drew me in as she said something. I kept watching her lips move, in fact they moved and rotated in the same manner, the same way a couple of times, and then I realized she was... SAYING MY NAME!

Father...Father...Father...Father, are you going to try your hot cocoa? You do remember liking my hot cocoa don't you Father?

Wh....What? Oh yes, Tammy, I'm sorry, I was just...had my thoughts...trying to....well, I was off in what my mother called "la-la land!" I'm sorry Tammy; I didn't mean to upset you!

*Father...*she seemed to be laughing at me. *Father...its okay!*

The rest of the night went as it was with the same small talk. I enjoyed being in her presence, even when she said nothing at all. I had thought over and over about telling her how I felt about her, but didn't seem to find the right time. She just seemed to need someone to talk to who understood who she was and what her views were. I found myself wanting to see her more and more and not understanding what was in store for me in the future. On one hand, she liked to talk to me, and tell me how she really felt; and on the other, I didn't know her to date, so perhaps her confidence in me had something to do with the fact that I was still, indeed, a priest. It could be that this 'safety net' is what kept her talking to me, as I know how hurt she was from her past.

Even though she no longer seemed to be living in her past, I knew that somehow it seemed to follow her wherever she went.

I walked home alone after receiving a hug from her. We had hugged, and I was curious if she always hugged me, or if she was showing me appreciation or pity. I wasn't sure and with all the questions in my head tonight, it wasn't the time to ask.

CHAPTER 8

The next day, I decided to stay in my room at the rectory, without really saying much to anyone, and pray. I was completely confused about what to do next. I didn't know how I should or should not feel. I was a man in a priestly form. I was raised a priest, I was trained to be a priest. Here I was with thoughts of a woman, a rosary maker, of all people who had been hurt so deeply, she trusted me BECAUSE I was a priest... not AM a priest, but was. If being a priest was the best part of me, then the best part of me was gone. I was struck by lightning, an act of God. I wanted to serve him and do his deeds, but now he was asking far more than I would be allowed to give. I feared that the next damage done would be to Tammy, and I wanted to help her, not hurt her. I wanted her to love me, not dislike me. I decided that I should give myself a punishment, in hopes that somehow things would get better. Except for water, I drank nothing else, and I pretended the water satisfied my hunger pains, as I could smell all that the housekeeper was making for the priests and bishops that lived in the rectory with me. All I wanted was to know which way to go. All I knew to do was pray and hoped God heard me. My prayers continued...

The Third Joyful Mysteries, The Nativity...

Our Father who art in heaven, hallowed be Thy name; Thy Kingdom come; Thy will be done on earth as it is in heaven. Give us this day our daily bread; and forgive us our trespasses as we forgive those who trespass against us. And lead us not into temptation; but deliver us from evil. Amen.

Hail Mary, full of grace, the Lord is with thee; blessed are you among women, and blessed is the fruit of your womb, Jesus. Holy Mary, Mother of God, pray for us sinners, now and at the hour of our death. Amen

Hail Mary, full of grace, the Lord is with thee; blessed are you among women, and blessed is the fruit of your womb, Jesus. Holy Mary, Mother of God, pray for us sinners, now and at the hour of our death. Amen

Hail Mary, full of grace, the Lord is with thee; blessed are you among women, and blessed is the fruit of your womb, Jesus. Holy Mary, Mother of God, pray for us sinners, now and at the hour of our death. Amen

Hail Mary, full of grace, the Lord is with thee; blessed are you among women, and blessed is the fruit of your womb, Jesus. Holy Mary, Mother of God, pray for us sinners, now and at the hour of our death. Amen

Hail Mary, full of grace, the Lord is with thee; blessed are you among women, and blessed is the fruit of your womb, Jesus. Holy Mary, Mother of God, pray for us sinners, now and at the hour of our death. Amen

Hail Mary, full of grace, the Lord is with thee; blessed are you among women, and blessed is the fruit of your womb, Jesus. Holy Mary, Mother of God, pray for us sinners, now and at the hour of our death. Amen

Hail Mary, full of grace, the Lord is with thee; blessed are you among women, and blessed is the fruit of your womb, Jesus. Holy Mary, Mother of God, pray for us sinners, now and at the hour of our death. Amen

Hail Mary, full of grace, the Lord is with thee; blessed are you among women, and blessed is the fruit of your womb, Jesus. Holy Mary, Mother of God, pray for us sinners, now and at the hour of our death. Amen

Hail Mary, full of grace, the Lord is with thee; blessed are you among women, and blessed is the fruit of your womb, Jesus. Holy Mary, Mother of God, pray for us sinners, now and at the hour of our death. Amen

Hail Mary, full of grace, the Lord is with thee; blessed are you among women, and blessed is the fruit of your womb, Jesus. Holy Mary, Mother of God, pray for us sinners, now and at the hour of our death. Amen

Glory be to the Father, the Son, and the Holy Spirit, as it was in the beginning, is now, and ever shall be, world without end. Amen

Oh my Jesus, forgive us our sins, save us from the fires of hell; and lead all souls to heaven, especially those who are in most need of Thy mercy.

The Fourth Joyful Mystery, The Presentation...

Thoughts in my head weren't getting any better. It was starting to concern me a great deal. I kept praying all day. I drank only water, ate nothing as my self-punishment. Later on that evening, I went to bed early. I was able to dream, and I did...

{*I was walking along the roadside of a dark cloudy day. I was in a rural area where there were a cluster of houses. The largest house had a fenced-in back yard. In that large yard, I saw a lion. This was not (or I didn't think it was) the same lion I saw before with the majestic mane. This lion was lying around doing whatever. It was acting like a common domestic dog. It concerned me, so I walked up to the fence and talked to it. The lion didn't respond, or chose not to, it wasn't made clear if it understood me or not. I was wondering if this is the lion that I hoped had all the answers. I was beginning to think otherwise. I saw a crow in the backyard on some kind of lawn ornament. It just looked at me. Its eyes were sharp and golden. It looked at me, just staring for a while. I waited for it to speak, but it said nothing. I waited some more. Still nothing. Not understanding, I kept walking, only this time the lion saw me and walked over to the fence. I looked across the street for a moment and noticed a fenced in yard with an animal looking at me. Stepping back, the entire neighborhood had fenced in yards with exotic or strange animals. I felt, as they looked at me, as if I were the one in the cage. I felt as though I were some animal in a zoo, being watched/observed. It was a lot to deal with. I was hopeful for answers. I wanted this lion to talk to me as the last one did, or the bird to have similar features as the broken winged bird in my past dream. It was confusing, and leading me nowhere. I couldn't decide if I should just run or continue looking back at these animals. I wasn't sure what was going on, as this didn't make sense. I kept walking, while looking at the back yards as I walked by. For miles I could see exotic and strange animals. I saw a peacock and its peafowl, along with a leopard, jaguar, elephant, and a family of skunks. Seriously, who has an entire family of skunks? I was more and more confused. What really was starting to bother me was the lack of people that were here. In fact, I was walking for miles in my dream looking for the people to these homes. No one seemed to exist. If they did, they weren't making themselves known to me. I had hoped that Tammy would be in this dream as she was in my former dream. I kept looking for her. I was hopeful that she would be here to be beside me, so I didn't feel as though I was the caged animal. None of the animals themselves seemed to mind that they were in cages in people's back yards. That was the oddest thing. None of them seemed to want to leave their enclosures. I started to run, and without looking back, I felt as though I was being followed. I kept running until I found a grocery store. For sure there would be people in there. As I ran around the corner near the ice machines I stopped and looked at my reflection. I was an animal. Perhaps all the animals in cages were people too, who only looked like animals to me. Perhaps those that were peering at me were my parishioners. Perhaps I didn't understand what the fuss was about, or why they felt it important to be watching me. Maybe they were wondering the reason I was looking in on them.}*

When I awoke, I was upset and frustrated.

Again, I found myself on the computer looking up answers to my dream. This one seemed to be so off, it was like I knew something was wrong. Perhaps something I was doing, or not doing. I was beginning to understand that caged life-style living at the rectory. Perhaps there was something I couldn't understand or grasp about life. Perhaps I would pray for answers, and ask for more of an understanding.

I had decided to pray all day. I gave myself punishment, or at least fasted for a day. I stayed away from the priest/bishops who could sway my decision one way, and I stayed away from Tammy who (without trying) would sway my decision the other way! Somehow I had hoped for a direction to my future. Here I am, a virgin man, who after serving as a priest for 15 years can't remember how to pray without full concentration. I have a woman who trusts in me because I once wore a white collar, but yet my thoughts lead to a future with her! How mixed up is that? How could I look at her, without being looked at by those around me? How could I ask her to commit to someone who she once adored as a priest? How could she ever get herself in the mind-set? I had to wonder these things, as I was so searching for a truth that I couldn't find. To make things worse, it's 2 o'clock in the morning, and as I have yet to go to bed after the caged dream I had last night, I didn't want to dream any more than I had to today, as I wanted to find the answers first, and then deal with everything later. The more I looked and came up empty-handed, the more upset I became. I am now upset.

Prayers? Not now! Thoughts? Too many already! I felt mislead by this dream!

There was a knock at my bedroom door.

Come in. I said, hoping it was the answer I was looking for.

It was Bishop Hein. He pardoned himself saying...

It sounded as if you were having a nightmare; I could hear you three doors down. Are you okay Father Thomas...

Lance! I interrupted him...*My name is Lance. Please call me Lance. I don't believe I will be responding much to 'Father' anymore.*

Very well, Lance...were you having a nightmare? It sounded like you could use some help. I couldn't help but overhear things going on and felt that you had awoke from another dream.

I didn't go to sleep yet tonight. I'm trapped in thought still about last night's dream. I'm having a difficult time with everything Bishop Hein...

Donald...he corrected me this time...my name is Donald. You are welcome to call me Donald, if it helps.

Okay, Donald, as you know, I didn't eat yesterday. I drank only water, and I stayed in private prayer. I feel as though I am punishing myself as I don't know or understand what these dreams mean, or how to even go about looking for the answers. I have to talk to someone about these feelings I am having, and I have to say that one particularly is leading me away from ever going back to the priesthood. It is leading me in a direction I am sure I hadn't ventured to before. It's all about her, and I have no direction to lead my heart in, or even if it should be lead into her direction.

Lance, you don't remember how to be a priest. You are in love with a woman who could use your affection. I don't know why you are complicating things for yourself. Soon you will be free to do what you want. If you want a job, go get one. If you want your own apartment, go get one. Really, Lance. It's a perfectly normal feeling to have. One shouldn't fear intimacy. God created it for those who he puts together. I don't have all the answers Lance, no one does. You have to do what's right for you; and hope and have faith that God approves.

Why did I become a priest then? My question was bold.

Trust in his timing Lance. Only he sees the big picture in our lives.

Why did I become a priest? I asked again.

Maybe this isn't about you, perhaps it's about her! She wouldn't have trusted you with her annulment and all the abuse if you weren't a priest! She wouldn't invite you into her home if you weren't a priest! She doesn't do that with anyone else… maybe this isn't about YOU! Trust in God's timing! Trust in him Lance. Allow him to guide you. Pray, yes, then listen. That's how it works best. Instead of worrying how you are going to tell her, if you are going to tell her; you should be asking yourself if you have what it takes to heal all her wounds!

What? What did you just say? I was really getting bold!

I'm just asking a question to you. Say she is in your life… You must be able to do more than give her physical comfort. You will have the responsibility to heal all her wounds. I was just asking a question. Make sure this is something you want and can deal with. Without being in a relationship, I understand all your excitement. Please give it some more thought and trust in His timing. I hope I have helped a least a little bit. I better get back to sleep. I have 6 o'clock morning mass tomorrow morning. Goodnight Lance.

I wished him goodnight as he closed the door behind him. He explained it all right there in a nut shell. My answer would come from my mentor, my teacher, and my friend. I was glad we had that talk. It was good to finally talk it out loud. I would need to talk more about both dreams, especially after how he said word-for-word what the majestic lion asked me in my dream, and how Tammy must have been represented by the broken winged bird. It was making sense to me, and for once since the lightening incident, I was more prepared in which way I was going to lead my life, and a better understanding in how I was going to live it. I could heal her wounds, and I wanted to take care of all the ailed her. I had yet to understand the more recent dream. It was really a question in my mind, because I was wondering to myself if it was a warning of some sort. Perhaps more would come to me in the morning. For now, it was time to get some more sleep.

◦─◦❦◦·─────◦❭◦❬◦·▸──────◦❧◦─◦

CHAPTER 9

I was wide awake at 6 am mass the next morning. I noticed the sun was shining. I somehow hadn't noticed it before now, at least not as brightly shown as it was today. The sunshine was showing through the stained glass windows of St. Michael's church. I sat in the front row, as I had after I decided to step down from my position as a priest. Today, however I was dressed in my black suit, with white collar, as directed by Cardinal Jefferson. Even though I was no longer a part of the mass, it was still important that I dress appropriately in church. I believed that it was the church's way of hoping things would just come back to me one day. As I heard Donald's... (Excuse me - I should address him properly in church) Bishop Hein's sermon on living a life with God in your heart, how much more relaxed and happy I felt. I somehow allowed God to take back control of my life, as if I were actually in charge of it, at some point. All things happen for a reason and I was pleased to finally allow a better understanding of my life, into my heart, and to know and understand how and why things were happening to me. Did I still need time to talk to Tammy? Oh, sure I did, but I now knew that I could tell her with all my confidence. I no longer felt as though I was being punished by God. Things would be different, but better for the both of us, hopefully in the end; and I expected things to work for the better for the rest of my life and hers. It seemed as though I would be getting my happily ever after ending.

Church ended, and after genuflecting in the aisle, I turned to see Tammy and Emily at mass, obviously before getting their day underway. Someone different was sitting with them. A gentleman. I was curious. I secretly wanted this new person in their lives to be related to them, somehow. I was in prayerful hope as I approached them.

Good Morning to you both...excuse me, to the three of you. I was expecting an introduction. Instead I received...

Oh, Good Morning Father! Tammy was polite and cordial, as usual. *We must get going, as we need to make sure Emily isn't late for school.*

And we need to get to work on some things, Tammy, the gentleman spoke up, as he genuflected and walked them out of church ahead of me.

I walked out just behind them, however their steps were much quicker than mine this morning. The fact that she still referred to me as 'Father' seemed rather troublesome to me this morning. Who was he, and why was I not introduced to him? Perhaps he wasn't important in their lives, or perhaps I wasn't. Doubt sank in again, and I wasn't able to think clearly the rest of the day. I was experiencing something different, not like depression, but similar enough to it.

After a few weeks of seeing them together at church, he arrived at the rectory door alone one day to see Bishop Hein. I was there at the moment, and was excused out of the room for private conversation. I was secretly hoping that he wasn't preparing himself for marriage with her. That would be another obstacle that I didn't need to deal with right now. I had been thinking, rethinking, and hashing out in my mind what to do, how to feel, and if and when I were ever given the opportunity to see her alone again. I rarely saw her anywhere anymore, and it was starting to worry me. In fact, she wasn't at the most recent market selling rosaries as she had in the past. Perhaps this gentleman was helping her financially. Certainly it would make things easier for her, however I secretly wanted that moment with her. I wanted to give her that opportunity to say how I felt, and if she were even interested in hearing it from me. I silently asked for an answer. When would I see her? When could I talk to her?

Thursday.

I quickly turned around. It was Bishop Hein. He said again...

Thursday. Hopefully that will make you to stop pacing back and forth like a caged animal, he said with a chuckle. *He set an appointment to come and talk with me on Thursday. He will be coming alone. I know how you and I spoke that night, and I realized you didn't get a chance to talk with her the next day, or since; so I know without asking you what's bothering you. I am not able to tell you what the appointment is about, only to say that the sooner you talk with her, the better off you will feel.*

He walked out of the room without saying another word. I'm sure he wasn't allowed to give me that much information, so asking him any questions would be out of line at this point. I glanced at the calendar, and I know Thursday would be a slow day coming, as I was eager to talk with her. I was in high hopes that she would be open for conversation.

Later that day, I received a visit from Cardinal Jefferson. It was the visit I was waiting for.

Father Lance Thomas, I would like to let you know, that as odd of a situation that this is, it was decided by the Pope to give you, your freedom from the Catholic Church and free you of all responsibilities of a being a priest. As your memory isn't serving you well, we further have asked the Bishops to speak on your behalf regarding your abilities and any paperwork that was necessary for this to take place. They did so in a very quick manner, and have served you well. Your accomplishments as a priest were highly noted, as well as your 15 years of service to the Catholic communities. I am giving you the option of living at the rectory, not only because your childhood home was given to the church as an orphanage, but because of the clause in the agreement that simply stated that the church is to care for the orphans and the home as long as you are a priest. It would be with much regret that those children would no longer have a place to live. Therefor it has been decided that since you are without a job to care for them yourself, that we would continue that service, until the day should come that you should feel differently, and ask to care for them yourself. In addition to this, we decided to allow you to live here at the rectory as this has been your home for so long. The priests and bishops don't mind, as they consider you a part of their family; and as long as you are not bringing home lady friends as a way of teasing or tempting their priestly vows. As you may or may not remember, that behavior is not tolerated. You are welcome to remove your white collar when you find it to be most comfortable, however since you are no longer a priest; we agreed that it would be better sooner, rather than later. Do you have any questions?

I didn't have anything to ask or say. With that, he left.

Thursday came and I found myself watching out the window like an eagle spying for prey. A car pulled up and an older woman got out, clenching a Kleenex. I imagined that she must have been the recent widow, making arrangements with one of the priests. I knew Tammy's friend had a late morning appointment, but waiting was difficult. My mother used to say "Watch the pot that never boils". How that was turning out to be true. I later found out that Tammy's friend's name is John Paulson. I had spent all day looking up information on him. He didn't have a clean record, and I was concerned for Tammy and her daughter Emily. Sometimes it's easy for a woman to get caught up in the same type of relationship, abusive or not, like she had before. I knew what she had previously been through before, and I didn't want that for her again; regardless of the situation. I wanted to spend some time alone with her, and I was getting more and more impatient by the half hour. I decided to take a walk to keep my mind focused, on what I was going to say, and to hopefully stop by Tammy's place on the way. The rectory was a busy place; as I was leaving two more people arrived. Out on the street, there was the usual hustle and bustle. I kept my feet walking, as I was finding it easier to think while walking. I was hopeful that she would want to talk with me, regardless of the fact that I was no longer dressed or acted like a priest. After walking for an hour, I noticed a little red car drive down the road, and glancing, I realized it was John Paulson, Tammy's new friend. He was alone, and I kept walking; now even more eager to see her. I knew my time was precious with her, and I didn't want to waste another minute. I walked faster as my feet hit the pavement harder and harder. I arrived at Tammy's place in what seemed like an eternity. I knocked and no one came to the door, even though her car was in the driveway. I walked around the back of her place only to find that the back door was locked as well. *Did she work today?* I asked myself, hoping for an answer. She co-owned a publishing company along the way of my route. It was no news that she was good at her job, however the demands of her family life with her daughter caused her to only take on part time hours. I started to retrace my steps back to the rectory. I had all kinds of thoughts and ideas going on in my head at the time. I was trying to stay focused on what I was going to say to her; however worry was now something that was creeping into my head. I don't remember her ever having to work Thursdays, however, that could change at any given moment's notice. I turned by the corner drug store and walked half a block to the glass front door of TAJJNT Publications. The name of the company was thought up by Tammy herself as the letters T - A - J - J - N - T came from her and her siblings first initials. (She was the first letter "T".) I thought it was very clever, and I was impressed with the idea. Going into the front lobby, I noticed how dressed up the lobby was. I remembered being here when it was just a used desk, with a coffee pot and a few lounge chairs in front of a table. Now the front desk had a newer look to it. The coffee pot was replaced with a coffee machine, and the lobby was decorated in the colors of chocolate and sage. Very nicely furnished. Impressive, inviting, and relaxing. I walked up to the front desk and asked if Tammy was in her office. I was directed to a lobby lounge chair, as her secretary went upstairs. Before long, she walked downstairs, with Tammy right behind her. I was thrilled to see her, however was concerned when I saw that look on her face.

Hi! I'm scheduled to be in a meeting soon, so I can't be long. How have you been? She asked me in a very professional voice.

I'm well Tammy. I hope everything is going well for you. I was calm. *Can I see you in private?* I said very boldly.

Sure, but remember I have a meeting soon, she hurried.

Getting into her office was a private opportunity for me to say how I really felt about her. However as I had the thoughts running through my mind all morning, I could only react. When she closed the door behind me, I wrapped my arms around her and kissed her. It was all that seemed right at the time. My lips pressed into her lips, and I could feel her suck in a breath. As I began to slowly form another pucker on her mouth, she also started to pucker into my lips as well. We were kissing. It was one of the most pleasurable moments of my entire life, that I could remember. We continued to press into each other's lips, until she parted hers slightly, enough for me to gently enter her mouth with my tongue. The taste on her lips was lip gloss, while the taste in her mouth was hot cinnamon. I was so happy to feel her wanton reaction that it didn't occur to me that I didn't even ask to kiss her; I just went into kissing her like some food-starved animal. When the kiss concluded, she stood there, still not inhaling a breath until I inhaled one myself. She was in shock, it seemed; surprised for sure. I spoke first.

I love you, Tammy; and I'm sorry if this bothers you. I want to get to know you better, and I want to continue to see you more often.

She didn't react. She seemed to be stunned. I suppose after getting to know me as a priest was quite different from who I am or wanted to be now. Just as she was about to say something, there was a knock at the door.

Yes, was her reply.

Tammy, the meeting is about to start! It was her secretary.

I gotta go. I'll call you, or you can call me.

With that, she ushered me out into the hallway, and locked her office door behind her. She ran off to her meeting, without saying another word. I went into the lobby and asked to make an appointment with Tammy the next day. An 11 o'clock appointment was set, and I was pleasant as I left TAJJNT Publishing company out the glass front door.

⚜ ❯◉❮ ❧

CHAPTER 10

The next morning, I was wide awake before the alarm woke me. I hit the showers and was nervous as I had no idea what was going to happen today. I could still feel the warmth of her lips on mine as I smiled in the shower. The taste of her kiss was more than I ever dreamed of. She was the real deal, she was all that I ever wanted, and I was going to tell her more today during my appointment with her. Upon going downstairs for breakfast, it was obvious I was in a good mood. One of the priests suggested that he thought it had to do with Tammy.

How did you know? I asked him.

Everyone is happy for her, Lance! he said to me, *she's waited for so long to find someone who truly loves her, and we're all happy to hear that she is getting married.*

Married????? I was surprised, or perhaps shocked.

*That's what the appointment was all about Lance...*Bishop Hein explained. *They are to be getting married in a couple of months.*

What? She hardly knows him! I was furious!

It's not our decision Lance, now calm down and eat your breakfast. Bishop Hein was quite honest.....he continued....*I know how well the two of you get along. Perhaps she was trying to find the time to tell you.* His voice trailed off.

How could she get married to a guy she's only known for a couple of months? I asked myself over and over at breakfast time. Oh my! What if she's desperate or pregnant? Women have been getting married for so much more; however, they also get married for so much less.

After breakfast, I decided to take an early walk, and leave for TAJJNT Publications. It was a nice day and I could use the fresh air. *Married...* the word that haunted my thoughts. She was getting married to John, and she wasn't mine to have after all. She needed more than just companionship. If I would have showed her how much I loved her that hot cocoa evening at her place, I wouldn't be listening to rumors that she is planning a wedding with someone else. I was still a priest that night, and she wouldn't have been so open to the kiss as she was in her office. She hadn't told me about the wedding yet, and perhaps she was still thinking it over; as she <u>did</u> kiss me back yesterday. She <u>wanted</u> to kiss me back, and she did. I didn't ask her to, but she did. I wanted to hear this wedding stuff from her, not just a rumor that John shared with the clergy, and they passed it along second hand to me.

Looking at my cell phone, I was happy to see that I didn't have any messages waiting for me to listen to. After yesterday's kiss and this morning's news, I was a bit concerned that she might have called and cancelled with me. I know that I wouldn't have heard the phone with the thoughts of her pounding loudly in my ears. I noticed I had just enough time to get to the TAJJNT Publications appointment with Tammy. I took a short cut through an alley, to get there early, as I was eager to see her again.

I arrived just 10 minutes early, and checked in with her secretary. She was in her office and would be with me shortly, so I took a seat in the lobby until she would send for me. I picked up a magazine that I noticed on the table before me. It was a bridal magazine. I looked through it and saw all the bright white bridal gowns. Some were sleeveless, some were long, some were short, and some had beading, while others were layered in tulle and lace. Some of them laced up the back, while others had a series of buttons that traveled from the upper back to the bustle of the train. All were gorgeous, no doubt; and with a gorgeous price-tag, I was sure with brand names I couldn't remember, or pronounce. Putting the magazine down, I noticed Tammy coming down the stairs to greet me herself. She found a place to sit down beside me, and was very pleasant.

Father....I mean, Mr. Thomas, it's good to see you again!

Tammy, always a pleasure, of course. Yesterday was a nice visit in your office; may we visit in your office again today? I said to her in hopes that we weren't going to talk out among other people who were coming and going in the lobby.

Of course Mr. Thomas, if you'd be kind enough to escort me to my office. Right this way.

She led me up the stairs into her office, where we could be alone to talk this over. Closing the door behind me, I took a seat in front of her desk. She sat in her chair behind the desk, and was all prepared to have a thorough conversation.

She decided to start...

Lance, I want you to know that I enjoyed your visit yesterday and have had many thoughts regarding what happened between us. I should not have allowed it to last as long as it did, and I'm sorry. You are new to this kind of thing, and I'm sure you were just a bit too happy to see me.

I love you, Tammy! I was quite abrupt. *There is no need to do this to ourselves. I want you, and I am guessing by your actions that you want me too.*

Lance, I do want you in my life, you are one of my closest and dearest friends. You baptized my daughter and you have been with me through all the tough stuff, so I need you by my side, I'm not going to beat around the bush about this. Yesterday's kiss made me rethink some decisions that I have recently made.

Like getting married? I asked her, and her face froze.

Yes, like getting married. Until yesterday's kiss, I was sure that John was the one who could make me happy. Emily and I have been on our own for a long time, and it has taken me a long time to get over everything that my ex-husband has done to me. So, I was thinking that John was the answer; however, I now am re-thinking the marriage idea. I have not told this to John as I don't feel as though he needs to know what happened between us. He is a decent man who had a few bad run-ins when he was younger too.

He was the bad run-in Tammy. I interrupted her, to clarify. *He hurt other people; YOU were the one getting hurt in the past, not him. There is a difference. Now, I have known you for as long as I can recall any church memories. I know how difficult it is that you and I were once* associated through the church, and am now standing outside of that part of the relationship. It's not easy for me either, but when I held you in my arms, I knew right then and there I wanted you. This is my fault for not saying anything sooner. I had planned to talk to you after church one morning, and then I turned around and saw you with John. I was hoping for an introduction...

I know Lance, that was my fault! I should have introduced you to him, but I didn't want to go into all the who's who and where did we meet, kind of thing. We met on Catholic Match, an on-line dating service, and I didn't feel as though you would want to hear all that, also, I didn't feel as though it was everyone's business. I felt bad enough having to go on a dating site on-line because no one around here wanted me, or the past drama, or the "baggage". Can you believe it; they actually call Emily 'baggage'? Why do people act like that?

Tammy, would you ever consider getting married to ME? I want you to marry me! Please marry me instead of John. I can be with you side-by-side...

Lance, I already said YES to John! Now what? You think one kiss can change all this?

You said that it was making you re-think things. So, re-think things! I can wait. I will wait as long as I have to as long as the answer you give me is YES!

Please let me give it some thought. Please give me some space!

Space? I know you as a priest, not that I remember that - so we never got to know each other like this. I stand back like an idiot as you okay to marry some guy you met on-line and haven't known for very long, all because he accepts your dark past, where YOU were the victim. So, after knowing me long enough to baptize your daughter, you are questioning my nature and wondering if I can give you some SPACE as you decide on what you should do? I was clearly getting upset. I didn't know why I was so angry with her, however somehow I was.

Seriously, PLEASE calm down. There is no reason to get so upset. It's not like I've had much time to think about this, as you just kissed me yesterday. Lance, did you expect me to take that new information and throw away all that I wanted to achieve with John? I really didn't know you were having these feelings about me.

Well I was, I pouted like a two-year-old to get her attention, however I remembered the fact that she was a mother who had already gone through that stage with her daughter, and I knew it wouldn't work, yet it was worth the try.

I don't have time for this Lance, she interrupted my thoughts. *I have another appointment coming in, and NO it isn't John. I will give it some more thought. Emily has a band concert tonight, the last of the school year; at 7 o'clock, and John can't make it, so you are welcome to come and enjoy it with me. We can talk some more then; however we will be in public.*

I look forward to it. I will see you later, I said while standing up.

I noticed she came around the desk to give me a hug, and I welcomed it. I leaned in to kiss her, and she politely accepted, but nothing like yesterday's kiss. I tried again, and she offered the same potent kiss.

Relax.. I whispered to calm her as I leaned in for the third time. This time, the kiss took affect over her, and she released a sigh as she returned my kiss. Our lips parted way for the moisture in our mouths to glaze our kiss. I felt her relax as we allowed ourselves to get lost in each other's arms. This was all the heaven I needed. If this deed, this one deed would send me to purgatory for all eternity, I would tell Him, that it was all worth it.

We released our embrace and stood there looking into each other's eyes for just a moment. I could see how she needed more time to think things over. I didn't want to be the one to break our gaze, but I knew her next appointment must be waiting for her by now. I didn't want to seem rude...

I know you have another appointment, so I won't keep you. Please take as long as you need, but please be in touch. I look forward to seeing you tonight. I love you...

It hurt to walk away from her, but if I would have overstayed my welcome, then I know she would have found me more annoying than sincere. I really did love her, and I didn't want to hurt her, or her daughter.

Later on that evening I met her at her place so I could drive the three of us to the band concert. I borrowed one of the rectory vehicles, an SUV, black of course; nice, clean, sporty, yet elegant. Her daughter Emily talked on about the 3 pieces of music that the band would be playing, and how much she really enjoyed playing the trombone. One of the songs was my favorite, Beethoven's Ninth. Beethoven was a genius as far as I was concerned, and I looked forward to hearing the band play that song. The other two songs that they were scheduled to play was Goddess of Fire by Steven Reineke, and Lightning by Todd Stalter. All three sounded good; however, I would be the first to admit that the last one would not be getting my vote as the favorite, even before hearing it.

The concert lasted 2 hours with contest winners playing some solos. I was pleased by the arrangements, however that Lightning song, still not getting good marks from me. Tammy and I hardly said anything as we sat and listened to the various arrangements that evening. Being by her side was calming. I could tell that the music soothed her. She looked relaxed, even glancing my way a moment or two. I was so glad to be with her, and I had hoped that she wanted to be with me, too. It just felt right.

The drive home was a quiet one, as everyone was getting tired. I was so happy that the night went so well. I was almost expecting John to take time away from his schedule to at least see Emily play, but he wasn't present for any part of the concert. I wasn't disappointed, but was wondering if they were.

I pulled up in front of their house, and turned off the engine. I got out, opened their doors, and walked them to their front door, making sure everything was safe for them. The house was empty, and the doors had remained locked all night. *Good,* I thought to myself. I had just wanted to make sure things were going to be okay. I thanked Emily for a great concert as she went to her room to put away her instrument. I leaned in to give Tammy a kiss, as she offered me her cheek. I kissed it gently and whispered 'Good Night' in her ear. She echoed my 'Good Night' wish to me before I left. I drove back to the rectory with Beethoven's Ninth still in my head.

CHAPTER 11

I woke up the next morning with thoughts of her on my mind. I didn't even get out of bed; I just laid there and thought of her. I thought of how she felt in my arms, how her lips felt on mine, and most importantly, how she seemed to want me to kiss her. He isn't her everything and I was beginning to realize that, otherwise she wouldn't have allowed me to kiss her. He obviously didn't make her as happy as she needed, and I was hopeful that I would and could be her everything. All I wanted was her at this point. I decided to go to the Lord in prayer...

Our Father who art in heaven, hallowed be Thy name; Thy Kingdom come; Thy will be done on earth as it is in heaven. Give us this day our daily bread; and forgive us our trespasses as we forgive those who trespass against us. And lead us not into temptation; but deliver us from evil. Amen.

Hail Mary, full of grace, the Lord is with thee; blessed are you among women, and blessed is the fruit of your womb, Jesus. Holy Mary, Mother of God, pray for us sinners, now and at the hour of our death. Amen

Hail Mary, full of grace, the Lord is with thee; blessed are you among women, and blessed is the fruit of your womb, Jesus. Holy Mary, Mother of God, pray for us sinners, now and at the hour of our death. Amen

Hail Mary, full of grace, the Lord is with thee; blessed are you among women, and blessed is the fruit of your womb, Jesus. Holy Mary, Mother of God, pray for us sinners, now and at the hour of our death. Amen

Hail Mary, full of grace, the Lord is with thee; blessed are you among women, and blessed is the fruit of your womb, Jesus. Holy Mary, Mother of God, pray for us sinners, now and at the hour of our death. Amen

Hail Mary, full of grace, the Lord is with thee; blessed are you among women, and blessed is the fruit of your womb, Jesus. Holy Mary, Mother of God, pray for us sinners, now and at the hour of our death. Amen

My prayer was interrupted by the ringing of my cell phone. I stopped praying as it was Tammy calling. I decided to answer it.

Well, Good Morning Sunshine! I was in a good mood to hear from her, only, it wasn't her, it was John.

I'm not your Sunshine, Father!...he was harsh sounding. *If you think that I don't know what's going on here, think again! Leave her alone!* He hung up the phone.

I just sat there, unable to respond, just to say 'Hello Sunshine', thinking it was Tammy; and the sound of his tone, that was something that bothered me a great deal. He seemed quick to anger and I didn't want that for her, in fact, I only wanted her to be with me. I was hopeful that she wasn't forced into telling him about what had happened. I was wondering what she would be dealing with if they were married. Did she want to get married to him? She was still re-thinking things out, as far as I was told.

I was sitting on the edge of my bed thinking of the situation, when the main doorbell rang. I looked out to see if I could see who it was, and it was John! Oh, Lord, what was going on that he felt the need to come here. It was obvious that he was upset! I heard the front door open and heard a ruckus in the main room. My name was mentioned, which meant only one thing, he wasn't taking this situation lightly.

My bedroom door burst open as John was coming through it, regardless of whether or not I wanted him to. He took two steps in my humble room, and had me backed up in the corner. The bishops and priests were out in the hallway, trying to calm him down from afar. He grabbed my tee-shirt that I had been sleeping in and shoved me against the window frame, hurting my left shoulder. It hurt to the point of throbbing, and I could feel my pulse in my chest. I was afraid that I would be dealing with more, in regards to John. [I decided to let him hurt me if he wished, as one of two things would come of it...either he would hurt me to the point of a head injury which might help me remember/regain my priesthood; or perhaps I would be able to use this situation to turn Tammy's head around, or at the very least, I could put a restraining order on him. One of these things was going to happen today. One of these things would be taking place by today's end.]

He rammed me again into the window frame and I heard something crack, either; my back, shoulder, or neck; not sure which, but a slow pain started to run down the back of my body. I was hopeful that he never laid a hand on her in this way, as she didn't deserve it. I wanted so much to make sure that he didn't hurt her, if this is what he was doing to me. I was now grinding my teeth together from the sharper stronger pain when I noticed the sheriff deputies coming into my room. John didn't hear them come in, and before he realized it, he was being launched to the ground and put into hand cuffs. It took three deputies to hold him down with the anger that he was dealing with. They cuffed both of his feet as well as his hands and they carried him out of my room by his limbs.

I on the other hand, was in pain, and not just the pain of my shoulder, but the pain in my gut that told me Tammy wasn't alright. If he hurt her or did this to her, I would be furious! I started to leave the room to check on her; however the shoulder pain stopped me.

Ugh!... I winced.

Lance, your shoulder... one of the other priests was in my room, looking over my injury. *You really need to get to a doctor! The bone is sticking out too far to NOT be broken.*

No!...He might have hurt her! I need to get over...

Lance, NO! Bishop Hein stepped in and took over the situation now. *You need to get this looked at first. If it makes you feel better, we will go over and check on her!*

I was drove to the hospital to get my shoulder looked at. Three priests were with me, as Bishop Hein decided to take a couple of priests with him, as well as a sheriff's deputy. All I could think about is her, and if she was okay. I bothered me beyond words how much I couldn't deal with the pain of losing her if something had happened to her. Thoughts of her continued to run through my mind. I was so concerned about her and consumed in thought I hadn't paid much attention to the doctor until he re-set my shoulder. The fresh pain was almost more than I could take. I doubled over in pain. Getting my shoulder wrapped wasn't fun either as a whole new set of pain pulses went through me. Finally, I was wrapped, iced, medicated, and sent on my way. Coming out of the hospital, I noticed Bishop Hein. His face was grim. He wouldn't even look me in my eyes when he said....

She stayed overnight in the woman's shelter. He hurt her pretty bad.

Which woman's shelter, do we know?

She stayed at the House of Faith, over on Keyesville Road.

I started to cry. I knew somehow that something was wrong. I insisted on going over to see her. The priests tried to out-vote my decision, however I was persistent. I needed to see her, and I needed to see her now.

We arrived in front of the House of Faith. I had to see her...I had to! Since I was with 3 members of the clergy, one being Bishop Hein; they allowed us to visit. There were four families staying there, however one was leaving, going back to her abuser. It hurt me to see her packing her children's belongings for the ride back "home". I had to see Tammy out in the living area amongst all the others staying there, house rules. I just couldn't wait to see her. She took her time walking out to see us, and tears came to my eyes when I saw her. She had been beat up pretty badly. She looked like she could barely walk as any strength that she had was gone. She probably couldn't get much sleep last night as thoughts of what could happen when she was sleeping probably filled her head, especially with all the she had been through and dealt with before in her previous marriage.

How are you? I asked hoping for a good answer, yet knowing the truth.

I'm fine now. Her answer was a simple one. It must have hurt to talk with one side of her mouth all swollen as it was. One of her eyes started to swell overnight, and there was a large gash over one of her cheekbones.

How's your daughter? I was concerned.

She's okay, a bit shaken and scared, but okay. He locked her in the bathroom before cornering me about your visit at work. He saw you leave that day. She was scared still, and I could see her hands start to shake as her lips quivered.

You're okay here, Tammy. He can't get in, and he can't hurt you here.

I was able to speak with confidence as no one came or went out of the House of Faith without being escorted. No one played outside, for fear of being seen or taken. If they were seen, they were moved to the House of Hope or the House of Love, both rural farmhouses that were way off the country road. A person would have to know where they were to locate them. Gardens were harvested and canned food was kept around in case someone was stalking and they couldn't leave for days. Very few livestock was kept to keep cost down, but offered enough hamburger to feed all three homes for a year or two. I understood why the homes were created and funded, however I wish they weren't needed. No woman needs to go through that ever.

Tammy, you've been through a lot, why don't you go and relax with your daughter, and if you need me, please give me a call. I will be here for you to see this through! I meant every word.

Are you strong enough? She asked looking at my shoulder.

Yes, for you, I am strong enough!

Do you have what it takes to heal all my wounds? She was serious.

Yes! I will help you through this. I will help you both through this. I will help us all through this! Yes, Tammy, I do have what it takes to heal all your wounds!

That was a question I have been asked a few times before, and the answer remained the same. I am here to heal her, to heal me, and become strong for each other, and with each other. Yes, I can heal all her wounds.

She went back to her room, where her daughter was staying with her. They refused to separate when brought in last night, as they had both been through this before, and knew how scary it could be. In their previous experience, Tammy's ex-husband would sneak in and hit her in her sleep. I understood fully what they dealt with, but couldn't accept, again in their lives. It was obvious that the wedding was off. I wished she didn't have this to deal with this, however I was glad she saw him for who he was, before it was too late.

His trial was short and sweet. Breaking into the rectory was quite the mistake as there were several witnesses to what had taken place that morning. All in all, John was charged with felony bail jumping, failure to check in with probate, three counts of domestic violence with intent to do bodily harm, along with breaking and entering, disorderly conduct, and since he was under the influence of drugs and alcohol during all the incidents, including the short drive to the rectory, he received his 6th DUI (driving under the influence); which basically sent him back to prison. Due to the violent nature of his attacks, he was placed in a maximum security prison out of state, to keep Tammy and her daughter Emily feeling safe. Eventually broken bones and bruises healed. The only scars left were those internal heartaches that only time can erase.

CHAPTER 12

Summer came and went, and by now, it was time for and all students to go back to school. The summer was spent in physical therapy, counseling sessions, faith-groups, and studying up on Catholicism. I didn't get to see much of Tammy or her daughter, as they were obviously dealing with quite a bit. They had sold their home and moved into an upstairs apartment overlooking one of the busiest streets in town, and just across the street from where Tammy's publishing company was. The apartment was a small three bedroom with all the bells and whistles: hot tub, walk-in closet, dishwasher, and laundry room. A lot of money usually, however she bought the building, with the potential to put in a sky-walk. It was easier for her to work from home as well, connecting with her Wi-Fi just barely across the street. Close quarters, yes, but could watch work from a distance, even on her days off if and when she felt the need.

There was some time for conversations, when I would call her to see how things were going, but busy getting ready for the upcoming school year, and needing those mom/daughter moments so their wounds would have time to heal. As for the upcoming school year, this year would be the big year, driver's education. According to what I was told, it had to be the most expensive class in school, but by far, the handiest. I didn't remember that part of my childhood, so I would listen to the excitement in her daughter's voice, or the worry in hers. From time to time I would see them out in the marketplace, either selling rosaries, or doing some browsing of their own. We would exchange a smile or wave, but no conversation really, as I remembered her healing from her former marriage, and knew that time takes care of most things. I was waiting for an invitation and one day, it came.

My cell phone rang. It was her.

Hi Lance! She was sounding happy-go-lucky today; and after her say my name, I was feeling happy-go-lucky myself.

Hey Tammy! How are things?

Great! Feeling good today! New books being sold from my publishing company, new secretary, and she's working out fantastic; and... my daughter is staying with my sister this weekend, so I was wondering...if... you want to come over tonight for supper? I'll make steaks on the grill, corn on the cob, my pasta salad you like, and lemon meringue pie...! Please say you will, it seems like sooooo long since I saw you.

Of course I'll say YES! That menu sounds like the best in town, and quite honestly, I've missed you so much. I love the talks and seeing you out and about, but being beside you is where I want to be.

Oh, good, can you be here.....? Uh.......Mmmmm.....well, whenever you want! I would prefer sooner than later.

How about right now? I can help you grill, if you'd like, & I would enjoy seeing you again!

Sounds perfect, Lance! See you soon!

I drove over to see her, and I have to say that I was floating on air. I was so happy to be seeing her again face-to-face, and in private, I wanted to sing from the highest tree-top! I arrived at her house, dressed casual as usual, and within the 15 drive-time as I hit every green light. She was wearing a lounger with a zip sweatshirt over top to cover her arms from any cool breeze that would flow through the open windows.

When I walked into her apartment, our eyes met. I had a difficult time not thinking about being held in her arms, and kissing her sweet lips. We smiled. I wanted to be good to her, and honor her as I should, but not seeing her, mixed with testosterone was an altogether different experience when she reached for me in an embrace. My lips found hers and we slowly kissed, simply, honestly, and lovingly kissed. I was in bliss! This is what happiness is, and I wanted to be part of it. The rush of feelings that came over me was more than I could take, and my lower body reacted oh-so-quickly, and I bumped my pelvic area against her upper hip. She pulled back, when she realized what I had just done.

Lance.... she said to me with a look of surprise and fright in her eyes.

I responded,... *I know, Tammy. I should not have done that to you. I'm sorry.*

*Lance, I'm just surprised that you could do that, I guess I thought, or didn't think that you could or would...*her voice trailed off.

I knew what she was thinking at that moment. Again, she remembered my being a priest, even if I didn't remember any of it. She was such a good woman; I feared that I would dishonor her in a way that would be unethical and uncalled for. Perhaps she was the one person that was keeping me sane. I would be needing to remind myself of that, apparently; and keep in mind that I was not able to act in a way that would do her soul any harm.

I think we should start the grill.... she said as she backed away from me. She seemed afraid. Perhaps, she's afraid of me? No, I shook that thought out of my head. Afraid of what might happen between us. She had to be having some kind of thoughts if she enjoys kissing me, after all, she allows me to kiss her. She just needed more time, so I thought it best to follow her lead with that next time.

We had the charcoal grill all fired up and working well when we put the steaks on. Slathering them down with barbeque sauce was mouthwatering, as we stood over them brushing it on. Time went by, with us watching vigil over the steaks, and before too long, it was time to get the corn on the cob ready. We prepared corn on the cob in aluminum foil and put pats of butter in the 'boats' we created in foil for them; to be placed on the grill. The food that we were preparing was making my mouth water, and I was looking forward to sitting down with her and enjoying a meal together. As much as I enjoyed her daughter's company, it was nice to be able to just sit down with her and have a pleasant adult conversation without hesitation. I think we both needed that, I know I sure did. Soon, it was time to eat.

Bless us O Lord, in these Thy gifts, in which we are, about to receive, from Thy bounty, through Christ our Lord. Amen.

Not a moment too soon. As we sat down to eat, I couldn't remember having breakfast or lunch. Perhaps I did, and I just didn't remember;

but I knew I would remember this meal, because it's always been a good one, and that I remember. The steaks were done just right, and just done enough for my taste, with that barbeque sauce slathered on, it was so tasty, I wanted each bite to last and last. The corn on the cob had that smoky-grilled flavor in addition to the butter that was melted all over each kernel. How the taste of those bites made me want to eat my vegetables more often. The pasta salad; which contained: macaroni, onions, diced ham, peas, finely chopped celery, and bacon bits; that she makes is flavorful and filling, so I knew not to over-eat it, or I would really be full. The dessert was the lemon meringue pie, my favorite, and that was her grandmother's 3 hour recipe. It took a long time to make, but was the best pie in town! Her grandmother really knew how to bake.

The after supper cleanup was quick, with no pans to wash, and few place settings, I knew it wouldn't take long, and I would be heading home for the night. Tammy washed and I dried, and we had our task complete before we knew it.

I have something I want to share with you. She looked at me so serious as she reached in the refrigerator and pulled a tall bottle out of the back. It was a bottle of wine, CRANBERRY WINE as the label read. She continued, *We went to tour a vineyard with my sister earlier this summer when everything happened....well, you know what happened...anyway, I love cranberry wine and hardly ever get the time or company to drink it, so do you think you'll join me with a glass before you go?*

We both knew it was getting late, however I enjoyed her company so much I didn't want to go home. I knew that if I stayed for a while it would get later and later, however I was going "home" to a bunch of celibate men who had no idea what I could be feeling at this moment. I wanted so much to talk to someone about these feelings, but I thought it best to enjoy the pleasure of her company. I gladly accepted and soon found myself sharing a glass with her on her living room sofa, looking into her eyes! Oh, how I wanted so much to touch her, or share with her how I felt about her, but all I could do was watch her sip her wine with her mouth touching the glass so gently and gingerly. I wanted to lean in and kiss her. My mouth had other ideas.

Will you marry me, Tammy?

I was worried of the look she would give me, so I barely made eye contact with her. She didn't say anything, and her body seemed frozen from shock. I glanced into her eyes and noticed that she was crying. There were streaks of moisture on her face where the tears once started to fall. She was smiling at me when I heard the word I had wanted to hear...

YES!

She exclaimed so loudly, my heart jumped in my throat. I was so happy that soon, I too was wet with tears. Oh how happy we were at that moment! This was what he was calling to me in my 'mishap' with the lightening. How could I have known this beautiful woman my entire life and still have remained a priest? I didn't need to know the answer; I only needed to see the result, with us, here and now. I was so overjoyed, and even more so with her feeling the same way. I leaned in to kiss the woman who accepted the miracle and fate of being my wife. How beautiful she is to love me for as long as she had, and all I wanted was for the two of us to act upon it. I didn't know how she would feel about it, so as with all other aspects in my life, I decided to take it slow.

Our lips touched and tasted each other's wanton desire as they danced together, with this feeling that filled both our bodies. Still overly excited, I push a bit more to touch her, and this time she allowed me to. My hands were on the small of her back working up her spine when I heard her let out a joyful sigh. I reached up farther and decided to play with her bra until I heard it unhook. I hadn't planned for that, however it was in the way of my rubbing her back anyway. I slid my hands up the back of her blouse where the bra clasp had been and I rubbed her upper back and shoulders as I continued to kiss her. I lowered my mouth to her neck and started to nibble and suck on the sides of her neck until she moaned out loud with desire. She was enjoying the attention and I had to admit that I was as well. I had never actually touched a woman, before her, nor did I ever remembering having a desire as strong as this one I felt at this moment. I knew how much I wanted her, and she knew it too; but nothing could ever replace the shame we would both feel if we went any farther. I kept kissing her, as she kissed back; but something in my soul reminded my mind of the forbidden desires of the human race, and how much we would respect each other if we turned back, only voicing our feelings for one another, not expressing them just yet. God has a time and a place for everything under heaven, as read in Ecclesiastes; and I was more and more understanding the words in which I had forgotten, even more now as I was living them. This woman who I fell in love with was one of my most trusted parishioners. She was the one I could count on to speak freely and tell the truth. She would be the one I would learn to rely on and depend on more than anyone else. I found her to be the one I would be with for the rest of my life. I knew it best to respect her as God would want me to.

Tammy, I love you, and that's why we can't go any further than this.

*But Lance...*her voice trailed off in shame, as she knew what we were doing was not seen as being accepted in God's laws. *I just want to express my feelings for you, but I know what you mean; we cannot go against God!......God!!....Wait, Lance, you are PREACHING GOD!*

I guess I am.......

Lance, you haven't done that before now..... perhaps...perhaps you really ARE getting better! Oh, Lance, I am so happy you have some of your memory back...again.

It seems rather odd how I am reminded NOW, at this exact moment how much I needed to continue to preach God's word.

Well, at least you are remembering more of what you want and need to remember. Although, I would have to agree that the timing is impeccable. It certainly is a kind reminder that everything has its own time, God's time.

Ecclesiastes!

Yes, Lance, I suppose that's the section of the bible I was thinking when I said that...Why would you ask?

Oh, just that I was thinking of Ecclesiastes myself just now, when I decided to pull back, and make it easier for us both to walk around with our heads held high.

She looked at me, without saying another word. She tried to hide the fact that she was tired. I could see it in her eyes. She attempted to hide her yawn as well, but decided there was nothing to hide. The wine was good, but was making us both sleepy now, as it was getting late.

I should get going back Tammy, as its late and....

No Lance, NO! We don't have to do anything wrong, but I would really like you to stay tonight.

I lowered us both on the sofa, and I held her. We continued to kiss and caress each other's bodies until we both couldn't fight the sleep off any longer. We walked hand in hand to the bedroom, where we would sneak kisses and whisper words of love and encouragement before falling asleep in each other's arms. We woke the next morning, still holding each other. I asked her again if she would marry me, and with another 'yes' answer from her, we decided it was time to move forward with our relationship.

CHAPTER 13

We were married on a warm day in June, the last available weekend for Bishop Hein to officiate. He was reluctant; however my apparent popularity made it easy for people to accept my new way of life, or as some called it, my new "situation". I was happy living with Tammy and her daughter Emily, who attended church regularly with me, as a family. We decided that we would take our marriage in the direction that God wanted, and that usually meant children, so we bought a house; next door to the orphanage, my former childhood home. Due to the clauses and legalities that surrounded the donation of my former home, I decided that the church could keep the house, as long as all necessary work that needed to be done on the house was done in a timely fashion. I became the Director of Operations of the Sacred Heart Home for Orphans, which I was paid a salary for. The great room of our home became my office, as I was right next door to the home. It was nice to not have to worry about the wear and tear of a vehicle. It sure saved a lot of expense. I had an SUV that was a donation from the church, so I could run errands, take children to the doctor, etc. I met with businesses that wanted to make donations, from time to time, such as clothing, or grocery donations. We enjoyed the opportunity to play "St. Nick" to all the kids at the home during the Advent/Christmas season, as some of the area merchants made donations of stockings, candy, school supplies, and toys. Things were certainly looking up for the orphanage. With Tammy's publishing company still doing well, we were financially stable enough to put away money for Emily's college fund, and buy her the car she wanted; a bright purple Volkswagen Beetle with a peace sign painted on the front of it. There were some splashed of color throughout the interior with flowers pinned up on the interior roof, each one representing a different friend. We were happy as things were going great for us all.

I still remember the day she came home from work with a smile on her face. I will never forget that day. It was late autumn, as most of the leaves had fallen from the trees. In the morning, your feet would touch a thicker layer of frost, almost to the point of being able to slip and fall. I was making chili in the big cooking pot for supper, which I enjoyed doing this time of year; when she came into the kitchen with the news…

We're having a baby! Well, actually two! Isn't that great honey?!?! She was excited. I was in shock! We created life!

We created life! I exclaimed as the reality of my thoughts finally hit reality! I could hardly believe it! We were adding to our family. Oh, what joy that was! Our love would grow into a baby – no – two babies! So much love between us, it created another baby, not just one; but two!

The babies are due in July. She said with tears of joy streaming down her face. She stepped toward me, and we embraced for a while with the chili still boiling in the cooking pot. Soon Emily drove into the garage, and a new look of excitement came over Tammy's face. I could hardly wait to see the look on my step-daughter's face. She always wanted siblings.

Emily's joy was silenced with tears when she heard the news, she couldn't even speak. Later we understood that some of the tears falling had to do with her not being able to grow up with them, as she wanted brothers and sisters then, more so then now. However, to say that she could still be a big sister, she was happy to help in any way that she could. There was only one 'clause' in the big sister agreement; that she be allowed to name them. We agreed.

Over the course of Tammy's pregnancy, we decided to take the time to educate the older children at the orphanage about marriage being one man and one woman, pregnancy instead of abortion, the facts of life, and the "birds & the bees", along with any questions that they may have. We picked an entire weekend to spend with them; along with giving Miss Mary the weekend off for her grand-daughter's wedding. We were next door to our own home, so it wasn't like we weren't home ourselves, in case one of us needed to get something from our residence, however we packed enough where I was sure that wasn't going to happen. I had an agreement with one of the pizza parlors in town, a buy one, get one free deal as he knew we would be purchasing a large quantity over the weekend, as the meal of choice (once a day) was pizza, and since we rarely did this for the orphanage, he knew that helping us out would help him out in the end as well. One of the feminine products companies gave free educational pamphlets along with samples of their new products in a teaching kit. Tammy was happy to find these items on line, and gladly talked with the girls about their body changes. She also purchased a single cabinet, painted pink from a garage sale in another town. The girls cleaned & hung it in the bathroom themselves, while organizing it with their 'lady treasures' as one boy put it. I talked with the boys about their changes and how to respect women and girls. I had received free samples of deodorant that I found on the internet, and was happy to give those out as well. The boys had decided to fix the backyard fence, so that was their weekend project as we talked. Emily handed out donations of toys from the two thrift stores in town to the younger children, as she read and played board games with them; who were still eager to see Tammy's growing belly. We spent the night there, so they could come to us individually with questions and afterthoughts from our discussions. We also took the time to pray a rosary with them nightly.

Hail Mary, full of grace, the Lord is with thee; blessed are you among women, and blessed is the fruit of your womb, Jesus. Holy Mary, Mother of God, pray for us sinners, now and at the hour of our death. Amen

Hail Mary, full of grace, the Lord is with thee; blessed are you among women, and blessed is the fruit of your womb, Jesus. Holy Mary, Mother of God, pray for us sinners, now and at the hour of our death. Amen

Hail Mary, full of grace, the Lord is with thee; blessed are you among women, and blessed is the fruit of your womb, Jesus. Holy Mary, Mother of God, pray for us sinners, now and at the hour of our death. Amen

Hail Mary, full of grace, the Lord is with thee; blessed are you among women, and blessed is the fruit of your womb, Jesus. Holy Mary, Mother of God, pray for us sinners, now and at the hour of our death. Amen

Hail Mary, full of grace, the Lord is with thee; blessed are you among women, and blessed is the fruit of your womb, Jesus. Holy Mary, Mother of God, pray for us sinners, now and at the hour of our death. Amen

Glory be to the Father, and the Son, and the Holy Spirit. As it was in the beginning, is now, and ever shall be, world without end. Amen

Oh my Jesus, forgive us our sins, save us from the fires of hell; and lead all souls to heaven, especially those who are in most need of Thy mercy.

Soon it was bedtime. The older kids, along with Emily had pitched tents in the fenced in back yard. They were picking tent buddies when we decided to go outside and tell Ghost stories, well Holy Ghost stories, that is. The younger children were on my lap, and on the laps of some of the older children when we talked about the mysteries of the Bible, and some of the times the Holy Ghost would appear. This was also time to answer questions about the angels or "heavenly beings" as they are called in the Bible. A fire ring was brought up from the basement, and soon smores were on the lips of all of them. It was a great enjoyable family-filled weekend that we all looked forward to, and didn't want to see end. The orphans were always well maintained and usually well behaved because Miss Mary didn't have time to deal with individuals as she was running everything herself. Once in a while, you would have one or two get out of line, but it wasn't for too long, usually. It was nice to handle the individual needs of each and every one of them over the time of a weekend. I was continuously grateful for all the donations and great finds that would make the weekend a better one, and help with those important talks.

Time passed quickly, and the closer we came toward the due date, the closer those doctor visits would be to each other. Upon one of those visits, we realized that the twins were identical, so it would be two boys or two girls. Upon hearing this, Emily chose the names as we previously agreed: boys names were Adam and Abel; and girls names were Hope and Faith. We found her choice of names to be very suitable and sounds that were very pleasant to hear. Emily added to the fun by letting the children next door pick the date that the twins would be born, along with whether or not they would be boys or girls. She even added to the fun by getting some prizes together, like homemade beaded bracelets and earring sets she made with leftover rosary beads, along with some rosaries for both the boys and girls. The local weight training center donated a small weight set to the boy who came closest to the correct answer. The library donated the series of girls' books to the girl who guessed closest to the correct date and sex of the twins. The pizza parlor agreed to their previous 'buy one, get one' deal; when the twins were born, making it affordable to share in the joy with everyone next door, when that day would arrive. We were so happy to be living in such a warm loving community, where God was so visible in our lives.

—⚒⸺ ⸺◆⸺ ⸺⚒—

CHAPTER 14

Soon the day arrived when we would welcome our twins into the world. It started out as any other day in the heat of summer. I was toasting bagels for breakfast when I heard the yells from the shower. Emily got up from the book she was reading to check in on her mom. She ran into the kitchen with a look I couldn't read upon her face. I put a bagel in my mouth as I put my shoes on, luckily I was already showered and dressed. I went into the bedroom to put the overnight bag into the SUV while Emily helped Tammy out of the shower & dry her off with a towel. I came back in, just in time to help Tammy get dressed in shorts and a tee-shirt. After sliding on her crocs shoes, it was time to dart out the door, locking it behind us. Emily was already on her cell phone with the hospital, letting them know of the situation and that we were on the way. While we drove, Tammy seemed rather calm, even though it was easy to see how uncomfortable she was. We were within days of the due date, so close in fact, the doctor was concerned that she may have to go on bed rest, however knowing how active she was, it was difficult to predict when this would happen. [Luckily Tammy's latest book was sent to the publishers and had pre-approval for the cover already, so the time she would take with the twins would be all theirs to have, while waiting for the book's release.] We pulled up in the emergency parking area. An orderly came out with a wheelchair to take Tammy into one of the birth rooms, and I sent Emily with her as I drove over to the parking area and found a decent place to park. I decided to pray for this wonderful glory that God had given to us.

Our Father who art in heaven, hallowed be Thy name; Thy Kingdom come; Thy will be done on earth as it is in heaven. Give us this day our daily bread; and forgive us our trespasses as we forgive those who trespass against us. And lead us not into temptation; but deliver us from evil. Amen.

Hail Mary, full of grace, the Lord is with thee; blessed are you among women, and blessed is the fruit of your womb, Jesus. Holy Mary, Mother of God, pray for us sinners, now and at the hour of our death. Amen

Eagerly I ran into the hospital. Inside, I asked about my wife and step-daughter and found myself directed to the 3rd floor where the birthing rooms are located. Walking through the hallway with bag in-tow, I finally found our room at the end of the hall, Room #331. Tammy was getting hooked up to the IV when I found them, with Emily timing out the contractions. From what I could tell, there was going to be no more walking around for her, as she was in need of bed rest. I took her hand in mine and told her how much I loved her, as she squeezed out another contraction. The pain was becoming stronger, I knew from the way she was reacting to it. Her eyes looked at me in distress, and I started to get concerned. Not having experienced this before, I didn't know what to expect. I would soon find out. The contractions came closer, until she was in a panic. The doctor had arrived and soon, all this would be over and we would be parents of two beautiful children, in addition to Emily, of course. The contractions continued and after what seemed like forever, we welcomed our identical twin daughters into this world. We named them Hope Margaret and Faith Mary. After the Polaroid was taken of the 5 of us, Tammy took a turn for the worse, and her heart rate started to slow. She must have lost too much blood and energy in the process of giving birth, and we were losing her. They called for the paddles and started to energize them as Emily and I were sent out of the room with the twins; leaving the doctors and nurses trying to revive her. My head started to spin as I didn't know what direction my life was going in. Did God want this for me? I asked myself that question over and over, until I remembered that this wasn't about me, or if it was, it wasn't JUST about me. She gave me two beautiful daughters, and now all I wanted was to be close to her. To hold her and to tell her how much I love her would have made the moment perfect. Complications were not what we expected, especially as she had given birth before to my step daughter Emily. She and I sat in the nursery with the twins waiting in silence until the doctor came in to see us, and gave me the news. I put my face into my hands and cried out-loud for her, hoping she would hear me in the adjacent room. I cried so hard, I could barely catch my breath. God spared my wife, but there were still some complications that would require an extended stay in the hospital. I was fine with that, as long as she was alive.

God bless you for doing what you could, and for saving my wife! I told the doctor and accompanying nurse who gave me the news.

I was so over-emotional by this time that I was sobbing, along with Emily. They saved her. It would be touch and go for a while, but they saved her. The rest of the day, Emily and I took turns walking back and forth from Tammy's room, to the nursery and back. All were resting, and I was at peace again. Family and friends were called, as they gave their congratulations over the phone, and started sending flowers and balloons. Emily called and talked with her friends at the orphanage. She pulled out the piece of notebook paper she had folded up in her pocket. According to what I was told, Koalton, the little boy I was fond of from the orphanage won the weight set, as he came closest in the boys' competition, with Teven coming in second winning a CD player; and Ella won the book set, with Poppi & Willa each winning some earrings and bracelets for a close second. I think that took Emily's mind off of all that had happened or could have happened today. I began to pray.

Hail Mary, full of grace, the Lord is with thee; blessed are you among women, and blessed is the fruit of your womb, Jesus. Holy Mary, Mother of God, pray for us sinners, now and at the hour of our death. Amen

Hail Mary, full of grace, the Lord is with thee; blessed are you among women, and blessed is the fruit of your womb, Jesus. Holy Mary, Mother of God, pray for us sinners, now and at the hour of our death. Amen

Hail Mary, full of grace, the Lord is with thee; blessed are you among women, and blessed is the fruit of your womb, Jesus. Holy Mary, Mother of God, pray for us sinners, now and at the hour of our death. Amen

Hail Mary, full of grace, the Lord is with thee; blessed are you among women, and blessed is the fruit of your womb, Jesus. Holy Mary, Mother of God, pray for us sinners, now and at the hour of our death. Amen

The next day, the baby pictures were taken, as I tried to select a good baby announcement. There were so many to choose from. I was overwhelmed, but Tammy was so exhausted from trying to breast feed, give time to Emily, and take time for herself, before falling asleep again. I decided that this was something that I could do for us, and it helped take my mind off of everything that sent worries to my mind. Waiting for her to wake up in hopes that I would get a minute with her was a lot to think about. I was feeling left out somehow, but I didn't want to be selfish. I did need her, but so did everyone else. We stayed in the hospital for a week, to make sure Tammy was well enough to take care of the twins on her own. Luckily I would be home to help out, as I took a paternity leave for about a month, still working on donations and overseeing the orphanage, of course; from the comforts of home. The baby pictures were loved by everyone and the announcements were well selected, according to Tammy. She was pleased with my selection and glad that I was able to take care of such things while she was in dire need of sleep. We quickly set up a schedule for the twins. Tammy had to do all the feedings, so I made sure we never ran out of clothes, diapers, wipes, or encouragement. Emily helped in the clothes department, as she knew more about what little girls liked to wear. It was going well, and I was so happy to have had Hope and Faith in my life, as well as Tammy and Emily. I was glad that I had made the decision to walk away from the priesthood; as I still had difficulty remembering it anyway. This was a much better life for me. Imagine all those who don't get to experience it, but wished they'd had. I too, wished they'd had. Fatherhood was the most fulfilling job in this world, and I now felt as though I must have mislead others when talking about the priesthood, perhaps, I must have even mislead myself. Now was a good time to pray for myself, pray for those struggling, and pray for those fathers out there who weren't sure how to be fathers…

Hail Mary, full of grace, the Lord is with thee; blessed are you among women, and blessed is the fruit of your womb, Jesus. Holy Mary, Mother of God, pray for us sinners, now and at the hour of our death. Amen

Hail Mary, full of grace, the Lord is with thee; blessed are you among women, and blessed is the fruit of your womb, Jesus. Holy Mary, Mother of God, pray for us sinners, now and at the hour of our death. Amen

Hail Mary, full of grace, the Lord is with thee; blessed are you among women, and blessed is the fruit of your womb, Jesus. Holy Mary, Mother of God, pray for us sinners, now and at the hour of our death. Amen

CHAPTER 15

Nearly two years passed. The twins Hope and Faith were now going to be two years old in a couple of months, and into everything! The Senior Prom came and went, with Emily going with one of the boys from next door. He and Emily were good friends and it was an early night for them both. It was so hard to believe that she was almost enjoying adulthood, and preparing graduating from High School this month. She planned to go off to a bigger college, but decided instead that the local smaller college was offering the same courses; and she was better able to take care of herself right from home. We didn't charge her room and board, as we didn't want to set her back financially. She was good with money, and I was pleased with the choice of company she spent her time with. She continued to work at the local pizza parlor, and paid for her gas and upkeep on her Volkswagen Beetle. I was proud of her and accomplishments, and most of all, I was glad to be her step-dad. There were times when Tammy would go with her to get party supplies for the graduation party, and come back with more items that they originally planned. Apparently more people said they were attending, and she wanted to make sure we had plenty for all. I was pleased that we were inviting everyone from the orphanage next door, as our lives mingled with theirs so often we felt as though we were one big happy family.

The day of Graduation finally arrived. We planned and planned, and added people and invited the neighborhood, to be certain not to leave anyone out. The Catholic clergy was all in attendance, as were the orphans next door along with friends and family. My sister Lili was attending a family wedding on her husband's side of the family. I understood as she had her family too. The graduation hall was beautifully made with the school logo carved into the wood trim throughout the place. It was quite impressive to see, and a nice touch. Truly, it was a beautiful donation by the industrial arts classes. Tammy and I took our place in the first row, as everyone was in alphabetical order. The twins were giggling on our laps, while 'Pomp & Circumstance' started to play. We stood to see the graduates make their way to their assigned seats. I couldn't be happier than at this moment. Emily smiled big as she walked with another girl, someone she attended some of her classes with. She had grown into such a beautiful young adult. I hoped that she and Tammy would remain close through the years, as they had been through so much together. After the graduates were in their assigned seats, we all sat and listened to the speakers. There were laughs and tears through all the speeches. The graduates had worked so hard to get this far, and they knew life was just around the corner. After the ceremonies were over, everyone met in the lawn for a group picture of the students. It was by far a moment I would cherish forever. I looked at the twins and I thought about how graduation would be for them, and hoped it would be similarly happy. We left and met back at our home, where I was put in charge of filling the ice bins under the tent that joined our yard and the yard of the Sacred Heart Home of Orphans. A small bus was coming around the corner finally finding its way to the orphanage, as all of them were in attendance to see Emily graduate. Some of the older boys asked to help and I put them to work right away. More coolers were brought out and some of the place settings were put in holders where the guest would start the food line. The chairs were in place, and I hoped we would have plenty of seats and plenty of food for everyone. I was glad to see that the Catholic clergy were in attendance with the rest of the crowd when the party was in full swing. I had mingled a bit with them, but not as much as I should, considering how well I knew some of them. I had Hope's hand and we were walking over to them when my life as I knew it, would change forever. One of the priests reached into his pocket to pull out his cell phone. That's when he realized that his rosary; that had been caught on a thread, or another item that gave the rosary its resistance gave way, flinging his cell phone out of his pocket. In doing so, somehow it was accidently flung onto the ground. It didn't actually fall on the ground; in fact, it fell onto the sidewalk, making that all-too-familiar sound of metal components & beads hitting pavement. I saw this happen as if it happened in slow motion, because at that very moment, I remembered where I had heard such a sound, only once before. Not only was I remembering that sound, I was also remembering the doctors telling me that there could be a simple thing that will bring back the memory that I had lost. There were plenty of suggestions, however no one thought about the rosary falling onto the ground that night. No one could have imagined what that could have sounded like either, nor had I before now.

Suddenly my memory raced me back to that night when I had been struck by lightning. I could see the dark ground and pavement all around me, as I lay helpless on the ground. The strong winds, large rain, and small hail pelleted down on top of me. My attaché and rosary lay in front of my eyes, when I see a figure coming to my rescue, coming to help me get some help. I couldn't see who it was yet, all I could see were the rain repellent shoes. As the figure came closer I could see that it is Tammy! My (now) wife was the one who helped me that night. She was the one who made sure that I arrived to the rectory okay, and then the hospital. She had never said anything. The rosary she gave me as a wedding gift was the repaired version of my own rosary which was originally my father's rosary. I remember the day that my mother handed it to me, the day that my father was buried. I remembered being at that moment, and I remember being on the sidewalk that night in the storm, and I remembered someone helping me; however all this time I gave credit to the clergy, but it was God working through Tammy that made me okay. Suddenly, I remembered. **I REMEMBERED! I COULD REMEMBER!** I approached the Catholic clergy.

I remember! I was blunt and loud when I talked to Bishop Hein.

What do you remember? He was asking me seriously.

When the rosary fell, I remembered that night when I dropped my own rosary onto the pavement, and I remembered that night, I remembered my life, and I remember the priesthood!

Now is a fine time to tell us Lance, look at all you have accomplished now!

I know, I know, but I wanted you to know that I remembered. How about getting me back in? Bishop Hein, you know as well as anyone how difficult it was for me to walk away from the priesthood. I think it would be a blessing if I were allowed to hold mass again.

Lance, the Bishop was honest as he looked down at Hope. *Do you really want to give this all up for the sake of the priesthood now? You have such a beautiful family.*

No- not GIVE it up, but to add to my already made happiness. I was serious. How could he ask me if I wanted to give up my own children?

That bothered me, as I looked down to see Hope glancing up at me; as I looked around for Tammy and Faith.

We will see what we can do Lance. I don't know what can be done. Let me get back to you on that. Bishop Hein concluded our conversation.

Weeks past, and we were planning the twins' first birthday party. The phone rang. It was Cardinal Jefferson. He was brief.

I am told that you remember things Lance. He said to me bluntly. *Is there something to want to share with me?* He asked.

I want to share it all with you Cardinal. I want to teach again, and I would appreciate the opportunity to celebrate mass again, this time, with my family by my side.

I see. He spoke simply. *This would have been easier to do, had you not married and started a family, however, with that said, I am happy that you finally remember. I have an idea. I have to be honest with you, this is a new thing that the Pope is doing, and not all the 'rules' are set in stone, so we may have a chance at it. Let me do some checking, and I will be getting ahold of you again. God Bless!*

With that, he was gone, and I was standing in our kitchen holding the phone.

A few days later I heard from him again. He was calling to inform me about the Personal Ordinariate of the Chair of St. Peter, and then indicated that he was sending paperwork to me regarding petitioning the Roman Pontiff. I understood that what we would be asking would be unheard of, and a complete stretch; however I felt it necessary, and it would be worth the try. I was nervous about talking to Tammy about it, but she was strong in her decision to back me up and support any and all decisions that I made regarding the Catholic Church. With her support, I watched the mail for about a week. The paperwork came and I filled it out as fast as I could, with Bishop Hein seated next to me in the rectory. I wanted to make sure that my answers were not selfish ones, and I had to be sure all was well within the teachings of the church. My heart skipped a beat as I could hardly wait to stand behind an altar again. I wanted to get back some of that I felt was my original calling. I knew in my heart that it was a long shot. I also knew that the long shot would be worth the try. Perhaps this is what my calling was all about. I wanted so desperately to know what God held in store for me, at least in the near future; however I also liked surprises, so having this take place in my life, I was so thrilled to see the final outcome, and I prayed that it would be an outcome I would appreciate.

———————————————————

A year later, after petitioning the Holy See, I found myself meeting before the delegates of the Personal Ordinariate of the Chair of St. Peter; lead by several Catholic Cardinals and Bishops, in addition to two representatives from Rome, as well as those responsible for the future of the Ordinariate. I had a meeting with them to better understand the process in which I was undergoing. I would be meeting with them again after a long and tedious questioning process that could take months. There were fifty clergy altogether, and I have to say that I felt outnumbered. I remember being nervous about my future with the Catholic Church, and Ordinariate. The process was an every-other day phone conversation asking me if I were still interested, and my reasons why. Each of these phone conversations were held by each member of the Ordinariate that were holding a decision, regarding me, in their hand. Each one, as with the step-by-step process, was to contact me via e-mail, via phone, and meet me in person. I was under careful instruction to make sure that I answered each question in full accord with the beliefs of the Holy See. One wrong answer and the case (as it was being viewed) would be taken out of the decision equation and would be nothing more than noted in a document somewhere with a decision to be a NO, with revisions to the Ordinariate's foundation to never be challenged again; and that was definitely against what I was hoping for. The Roman Pontiff remained undecided, and the fate of my future as a married priest with the Ordinariate lay in the palm of his hands. I couldn't begin to understand all that I would be asking, as the ink was barely dry on the Ordinariate formatted foundation paperwork when I served him with my petition. These fifty men, who I was required to meet with would serve as the Pope's judge and jury as he would come to a decision in the future. The time was now to make revisions and remarks on the Ordinariate, while it was still new and not all the details panned out just yet. I didn't know that one day I would be questioning what it was that I wanted out of life a third time. The first time, I was guided by the Holy Spirit to become a priest, and the second time; I was guided to be a husband and father. As far as I was aware, if/when I was granted such an honor, I would be doing several mission trips with my family; while being asked to assist in several masses before being able to lead a mass alone. I remained filing paperwork for my parish to become part of the Ordinariate, if I were allowed to take another vow. It was a tough decision, and I was ready for the challenge. It was what I wanted, and I knew I needed to keep pushing this forward.

My family backed my decision, despite the tension that grew in our home surrounding the outcome and my future and fate with the church. As the demands of the church weigh heavily on my shoulders with the constant contacts and paperwork, I could see it taking a toll on my wife and daughters. One day, I found myself home alone. It was a beautiful day, and they had decided to go to the zoo. Earlier that day, my daughter Hope called me *boring*. Well, to her, I just wanted to stay home. In truth, I would have much rather been spending the day with them; however, having to wait for phone calls was a part of the new process, and it was important for me to go through the process with stride. I understood that it was a strain on them, as well as me. It was a lesson in the demands of the church; I was sure of that. Tammy did her best to keep the girls occupied while I either waited for a phone call or researched information to file another paper. Did those fifty men each need to call me? I'm sure not, however there wasn't a protocol in place yet for former Catholic priests to join the Ordinariate. In fact what I was petitioning was certainly unheard of. The entire process was still a long shot, but still worth a try. Not only did each of them have to be present when I was to be before them, each needed to speak with me before hand, as to the questions he would be asking at the hearing; so it was important that each of them file all of their paperwork separately from each other. All paperwork would then be viewed by the Pope and a decision made at that time.

CHAPTER 16

As I continued to deal with the pressures of going on with the possibility of being a married Catholic priest in the Ordinariate, there came a point in our marriage when I was truly concerned for our married future together. I understood that this process was putting a strain on our relationship, but I didn't realize how much I had neglected and nearly forgot about my wife's needs, until the one day that everything reached its boiling point. I still don't know how I missed all those social cues from her, but I certainly did, and I now know how much I would have regretted it, had I never known. It all started one morning when I had spent the night on the couch. I had been waiting for a call from a bishop who had come into the United States on a late flight. He wasn't aware of the time when he called me, and apologized during the conversation when he realized it. He was the last phone call that was scheduled to call that week, and I waited for him, as I needed a day off with my family, the next day. I was desperate to see them outside of our home, as I knew they wanted to go out and have some fun somewhere either outside or out and about, perhaps a pizza night. The bishop and I had made pleasant conversation as we talked. I knew he was supportive of my decision, which was greatly appreciated as the others who had contacted me until now didn't give me any remarks either way. Anyway, everyone was asleep when I hung up from him. Feeling satisfied with the conversation, I decided to take a few minutes to sit down and look at some mail when I fell asleep on the couch. I woke to Tammy making breakfast in the kitchen. As I was walking toward the kitchen, she hurried past me to get the girls up. I didn't say anything to her as she seemed pre-occupied, however I wished I had. I walked back toward the bedrooms and could hear her waking Hope and Faith. I stepped into our room, and noticed our calendar on our bed. I wondered how it had gotten there from the wall on the other side of the room. Puzzled, I decided to hang it back up, when I did so, I noticed that there were not any little golden stars affixed on the calendar for this month. It is our marriage tradition that we note each day we make love with a little golden star. This month didn't have any, looking back; there was only one on the last two months. Suddenly I realized what the point was to the calendar being sprawled out as it was. She missed me, and needed me. Well, I needed and missed her too. I sat on the bed for a minute to think about doing something special with her, when I heard the SUV leaving the garage. Obviously she was worried I had another phone call coming in and decided to pack the girls and breakfast, and go to the park, again for the third time this week. I found myself alone. Very alone. I felt as though I had done something wrong by her somehow. Who knows? Had I went to bed as planned last night, things may have been different today. At first I had started to feel sorry for myself and our marriage. Then I realized that only I could fix this part of our marriage. I couldn't change things, but I could try to make them better. I took a quick shower and dressed in casual clothes. I grabbed the keys and my wallet and left the house, driving for the first time in weeks. Feeling locked up at home was starting to get to me anyway, and I needed the sunshine. Driving along the street, I could see the neighbors water their gardens, jogging, talking on their cell phones along the sidewalk, mowing the yard, or walking the dog. It was refreshing to see people again. I drove to the park where I could see Tammy's SUV. Parking next to it, I could see her and the twins having breakfast with a friend…a gentleman friend….and not one I knew. Every possible emotion ran through me as I saw them talking, laughing, and enjoying the breakfast Tammy had prepared. It hurt me to see her laugh at another man's jokes, and respond to him the way she so often responded to me. I sat and watched them. I don't know what the conversation entailed, however I was simply jealous because she was giving attention to someone else. She didn't cuddle close to him, or even reach out and touch his arm as she did me; however wishing I was with her at this very moment made me ask what I was still doing in my vehicle. I felt as though I was spying on my own wife, and for no good reason, except for the fact that it was me who was pushing away. I cautiously got out and walked toward them pushing the lock button on my key ring as I walked. I was almost near them when I heard Hope and Faith call me *Daddy*. My little girls were happy to see me out and about. Squatting down to get closer to them, hugging and kissing them, I was smiling again, and for a minute I almost forgot about the man sitting with my wife. I stood up and looked at her. She wasn't as happy to see me as I was to see her. I decided to introduce myself to the gentleman, letting my presence be known.

Hi, I'm Lance Thomas, Tammy's husband. I said very sternly, with my firmest handshake.

Hello Lance, Tammy and I were just talking about you and your decision. I'm Deacon Jeffrey Greenback. I have been in talks with her and the kids about supporting you, and making sure to be out of your way when these calls, that you must wait for come in. I hope I'm not out of line here, Lance; but I hope that things work out better for you than it has been. I used to be a priest, until I met my former wife, then wanting to continue working for God, I found myself a Deacon. If you aren't granted what you are hoping for, we could always use another deacon on our team.

Did he just say former wife? Perhaps he was being helpful, after being through some rough stuff of his own, and perhaps he was interested in my wife. Jealousy was cutting into me again, as I tried to keep it under control. He introduced himself as a deacon. Hmmmm…a deacon. I hadn't thought about taking that route, although I would consider it if what I was considering didn't happen for me…for *us*, I corrected my thoughts.

I didn't think of my wife and children as being in my way, Deacon Greenback. I appreciate your support of my and my wife's marriage; however we are fine. I'm busy for now, but will soon free up some time for family, and this difficult time will be past us.

I hope you are right Lance. It is never too soon to focus on what is truly important to you in this life. I would consider deacon hood if you get the chance.

I think I will if things don't work out in my favor for the Ordinariate, Deacon Greenback, I will consider doing all kinds of options.

I was concerned that Tammy hadn't said anything to support me at this point. I nodded in her direction.

Tammy, you and I both know how things will be once this will be passed or rejected. Remember all the support I had from you and the family?

Lance……I'm….. I'm not so sure about it anymore. I don't know how much longer I can wait…..wait for you, Lance. I'm waiting for YOU!

Her face was stern; her bottom lip started to quiver, and her voice was not as sweet as I had always remembered. I was starting to have concerns over how much the deacon knew of our marriage, and how she was able to find the one clergy member in the area that I didn't know, and then ask him for help. Oh, how I wanted answers right now, as I was so uncertain of our future. I was both, upset and angry as we used to be able to talk things out, but lately, I hardly ever saw my wife and daughters. I used to help people myself, and often had afterthoughts of whether or not what I would say would even get through to the people who I was trying to help. I appreciated this man's opinion as he was trained to counsel those who truly needed it, however I felt as though he were trying to take over for me, and that's what gave me such an uneasy feeling.

The girls, who were playing in a sandbox only a few feet away, and close to where were talking, decided to ask me to join them. It had been a while since I played in the sandbox with them, so I did gladly, while keeping an eye on my wife, as well as my daughters. I felt like the worst husband and father in the world. Here I was with a falling-apart marriage, and daughters who missed their Daddy. Luckily I was with the girls in the sand box; making a sand castle we called 'Heaven'. What I needed to focus on next was my wife, Tammy. I noticed that she continued to talk to the deacon while keeping her eyes on me. She didn't seem happy that I found them talking. Perhaps it was my attitude; or perhaps it may have been something that I needed to worry about. After a while, he got up and left her sitting under the park shelter by herself.

Let's go see how Mommy is doing, I told the girls after the sandcastle was complete.

Yeeeaaaah! They said in harmony as they ran toward her.

When we got closer, I could see the tears starting to well-up in her eyes. She looked at me in silence for a moment, and then she took a look at the girls. She put on the biggest smile I ever saw on her face. I realized at that point that what she was dealing with was more than just what I thought, as I saw a tear starting to stream down her face. It was obvious at that moment that she was smiling to stop the tears from falling. I felt like holding her and crying, however I remembered that we were in the park, and in public. It wouldn't be okay for the girls to deal with any dramatic moments at this time.

Let's go get some ice cream like we always do Mommy, Hope spoke first, followed by Faith; *Yes Mommy, let's do that right now!* She was pulling on Tammy's arm, attempting to drag her off the bench she was sitting on.

Yes girls, I said with my famous 'Daddy' smile, *let's go get some ice cream.*

You don't usually go with us Daddy, Faith tattled, *it's always that other man who wants to talk to Mommy and help her cry.*

Yes, Daddy, Faith is right, are you sure you know how to get there Daddy? Hope was concerned for her sister's request.

The information that they were sharing caused a lump to well up in my throat. I decided it was best to ignore the new information until we were home. I took them by their hands and walked them to our vehicles. The SUV unlocked when I was close, as Tammy had the lock button in her hand, as I had each of the girls by the hand. I put them in their seats in the backseat and I opened the door for Tammy to get in. Instead she handed me the keys as I stood by the driver's side door.

They need you. She whispered through her tears. Stunned, I looked at her. It seemed difficult for her to be close to me at this moment; and I realized that what she said about the girls needing me was right. I gently took my keys from her, while I pulled my vehicle keys out of my front pocket and gave them over to her.

I'll see you at home, I said to her directly.

Feed the girls a snack before you put them down for a nap. I need some time to think. She informed me. That was good enough for me. I just needed to know what was going on. Perhaps she would get it sorted out and come home.

I need you! Please don't be too long, I said to her.

She gave a subtle smile to me, waving and smiling to the girls; she walked to my vehicle and got in behind the wheel. Getting into the SUV I could smell her cologne with just a hint of honey nut cheerios, the twins' favorite snack. I left first, hoping she would follow but she didn't. She sat for a moment before leaving, and went a different direction altogether. Back at our home, the girls snacked on cheese cubes and apple slices before brushing their teeth and taking a nap to a Robin Hood movie. I had hoped that Tammy would arrive to see them crawl into their beds; however, she hadn't arrived home yet, and I was curious what she was out and about doing. Perhaps she just needed a moment from the situation to think things out. I locked the house doors and decided that I should get a nap in, as sleeping on the couch certainly wasn't getting any rave reviews from me. As comfortable as the couch was to sit on, it really did a 'once-over' on my back. I decided it would be best to crawl in our bed, getting naked first, then slipping in-between the sheets, just hours after my wife was in it, just a few hours ago. I remember feeling loved and cared for, as if sleeping in the bed sheets gave me a sense of feeling intimate. To me somehow, I felt the relaxed sense of happiness and I soon found myself asleep.

I awoke to hear the master bathroom shower running. I knew she was home. Looking at the clock, I realized I was asleep for a half-an-hour before hearing her. Getting up, I walked to the bathroom, and before waiting for an invitation, I stepped into the shower behind her. Turning around, I could see the surprised look on her face that told me that she wasn't expecting me. Taking the soapy loofah-sponge, from her hand, I lathered it with more soap and started to gently wash her back. She allowed me to nibble, kiss and touch her neck, hips and buttocks along the way as I washed her. Bending down, I washed her legs, and noticed that she hadn't shaved in a while, probably not getting enough time away from the girls to take time for herself. I realized how neglected she must have felt, and I had promised myself that I would make love to her. [Years back I pursued her, and she came into our relationship through me, as she would have never pursued a former priest. I had to make this right with her. It was my responsibility to make things right. I was hoping that she was feeling the love I had for her. There was only one way to be sure.] I turned her around in the shower, and my lips found hers. If she was or wasn't crying, it was unclear as the water continued to rain down upon us from the messaging shower head. Kissing her, I felt her resist me at first, as though she wasn't sure if I wanted her or not, or perhaps afraid to let go, I wasn't sure which. Deciding to push the intimacy one step further, I reached for her breasts. I knew that she enjoyed my touching them, as I did as well. She appreciated my gesture as she had some of her own as we continued to fondle each other in the shower. Our kisses were deepened, and then gentle again, then deep once more, as we continued this cycle of desire. We touched and fondled each other until we couldn't hold it in any longer. We stepped out of the shower together with our towels being wrapped around us, each by the other. We kissed and cried as we both came so close to losing something in the mix of our lives, we almost lost each other. We cuddled together on our bed as we continued our kisses and fondling there, still wrapped in our towels. Immediately, my mind raced to her, then our lives, our children, our families, and once more, each other. She stopped kissing me for just as moment as she searched my eyes for my thoughts.

Lance, when you are kissing me, can you make one promise...please?

Anything...I love....

Lance, I beg you to only think about me at a moment like this one. When you are kissing me, I can tell if you are thinking of something else, other than me. I don't know if all women have this ability, but I certainly do; so I beg of you to only think of ME when you are kissing ME.

My eyes welled up with tears as I felt her heart speak to me, through her lips, and I understood. I shifted in our bed, and removed our towels; mine first then hers as we continued our kissing, fondling, then our lovemaking. We both eventually reached our climatic moments, first her, then I shortly followed. Kissing deeper and deeper, we held each other afterwards, not talking, not saying anything for a while. We enjoyed being with each other as intimately as we could be. We really reached the higher ground today, in the way of our marriage. What if the communication barrier would have stayed around for longer? Perhaps there might not have been anything to save. We needed to take the time for conversation, a time to understand one another, and a time to continue our openness with one another. There was a time to talk things out, while we each had the other's attention. I was the first to speak.

I'm sorry that I haven't been a part of this for a while. I've been working so many hours with my Ordinariate petition that I've neglected the best part of my life, you and the kids. I love you Tammy. I am asking for, and begging you to find it in your heart to forgive me. I love you beyond words; and because of your love, I feel God's love much closer than ever.

I'm sorry too, she seemed truthful as she continued, *and I should not have talked to Deacon Greenback, instead of talking to you. He really had me going the other direction in an attempt to stay out of your way. Only now, I realize that we weren't in the way, just as you told him. I trust you, Lance, when you say that, because I've known you for so long. I love you beyond words. I think we should keep making this work. I'm not upset with you anymore, and I now know that you weren't angry with us. I just thought that I was doing you a favor by staying out of your way, I also realize that you need us here, as well as we need you. I seemed to have lost sight of that Lance. I do love you. I am so happy right now to be able to talk with you about this. We really are a team, and this all takes teamwork. Thank you for loving me, and thank you for making love to me right now. It was one of the most pleasurable experiences we have shared in a long time.*

Tears welled up in my eyes. She knew by looking at me that I was as sorry as she was if not more so.

I'm sorry Tammy. I choked out the words that would bring our souls together again.

I held her close and kissed her. The stress from the petition paperwork made its way through me as I continued to cry as we held each other close and kissed. I loved Tammy for being able to see the man I am, the man I was, and the man I wanted to be. I found her love to be as refreshing as a gallon of ice water in a desert. She was the one and only pleasure I needed on earth, and I knew at that point we could get through anything together.

Just then I heard the familiar noise of two little girls making their way down the hall to our closed bedroom door, I soon realized and remembered again that I was naked.

The girls! I exclaimed as I quickly got up and grabbed underclothes out of my dresser drawers.

They knocked. Tammy played the "who is it?" guessing game with them until they each stated their first, middle and last name; barely enough time to get dressed, but managing somehow before they burst the door open. She apparently had better dressing skills than I did, I realized as she was fully dressed, putting on her socks when they bounded through the bedroom door. I had barely fastened my jeans, wearing a crocked tee-shirt, with no socks when they saw me.

Daddy, you aren't wearing any socks. Where are your socks? Faith asked me.

Silly Daddy! Hope followed her comment, almost on-que.

Tammy told them how today we were going to be having lunch at the family's favorite pizza parlor. They were happy as they went to pick up their bedroom, the only stipulation. They hurried to their bedroom, as I kissed my wife at that moment, remembering why I married her in the first place. I winked when I patted the seat of her jeans. She smiled in satisfaction. I went to straighten my desk area, and turn off the computer. It was a good day to just step away from everything that seemed to invade our marriage. Tammy went to check on the girls, and to see what kind of progress they were making. That day was a glorious day for our marriage. We proudly displayed three golden stars on the calendar for that day. A day, I will truly not forget, as a turning point, held as a reminder to what was important to me and my happiness. From that day forward, I made it a point to always remember that day and keep it in the for-front of my mind, as I needed reminding from time to time, as the responsibilities of the Ordinariate petition made more of a demand on me, and on us.

CHAPTER 17

A few months later, I was ready to meet again in front of the Board of the Ordinariate. I was nervous, but prepared, as Tammy, Emily, Hope and Faith joined me that day. I wanted them to understand how I was truly serious about being a good husband and father. Further, I needed the Ordinariate to understand all that happened to me, and all that I had been through to make it to this point. As I looked back to see my family, I noticed sitting two rows back were the clergy in which I worked so closely with, including Cardinal Jefferson, Bishop Hein, and also joined by Deacon Greenback.

The meeting process took about a week, while all of my work was examined and questioned, both in my personal life, and in my life as a priest. As a clergy member, the board needed to get a copy of all my work, as to show seriousness about the sacraments, masses, and the importance of my previous position as a priest. Every marriage file was open, along with any and all therapeutic talks that I had with each married couple before and after the ceremonies. Every baptismal record was re-opened and examined for further sacraments in the church, as it was my duty to make sure that families who lived in our area were still attending church and raising their children as Catholic. All the Catholic annulments that I assisted with (including my now wife, Tammy's) was noted on file, to assure that all paperwork was handled with correct and proper procedure. All of my former mass servers, both boys and girls were questioned whether or not anything immoral or inappropriate acts had happened or taken place when they served me during each mass. Their mass assignments and schedules were pulled from the church files, and each and every server was mentioned by name as they participated; at their home parishes, with parents, several Cardinals, and all the local clergy present; in that questioning process as well. Every paper that I ever filed; as a priest, for last rights, funerals, First Communions, Confirmations, reconciliation time frames, and group meetings and sessions, were copied and sent to Rome for the file. All financial records, from mass payments, to bills paid while I was a priest at any and all parishes had to be examined for possible fraud. All the papers written while in the seminary at St. Francis was pulled from files and copies made to show importance of religious life. In my personal life, I had to show all the paperwork, financial and otherwise, in my home life, Tammy's publishing company; and work that I had completed with and for, the Sacred Heart Home of Orphans. All fundraising activities were noted and submitted into the file. The births of our children were examined, and notes from the doctors were important as to whether or not any more children were to be born of our marriage. It was vital that no birth control or the morning after pill was used to abort any unborn children, as my character truly needed to be in full compliance with the Catholic Church in order to even be considered to enter the Personal Ordinariate of the Chair of St. Peter. I found it most interesting that they needed information on all our family vacations, as our activities were noted as those activities couldn't be anything that was questionable, such as going to see mediums, spiritualists, voodoo masters tarot-card readers, or other activities that the church would have viewed as going against my own teachings, both, when I was a priest, and now in my own home. I had an opportunity to petition at that time for deacon hood, in case I wasn't allowed into the Ordinariate. I suggested that I would wait to see the outcome first before jumping into any new paperwork. Luckily any and all flaws that I had were not against God, my family, or the Catholic Church; otherwise they would have held the door open as they would have booted me out of the building. I realized how important this was to us. I knew that I was not the only one giving up my time through this process. I fully understood that the board members, the clergy that backed me, along with my parishioners and parishes, and especially my family; were also giving up a great deal of their time, all for my sake. I was hoping that none of them felt belittled or questioned my sincerity through this process. I would be a wait to hear the outcome. It was a long and anxious wait.

I was finally granted priesthood in the Personal Ordinariate of the Chair of St. Peter later that year. I was the first Catholic priest to be accepted by the Roman Pontiff and the Holy See. What helped my situation was the circumstances in which I left the priesthood involuntarily, almost against my own will. No other Catholic priest had received this honor, before or since. I would like the blessed opportunity to become a Bishop; however I understand that won't be possible, and I do not wish to push my luck at this point. I have to say that I was overjoyed to be leading mass again. I am looking forward to giving my daughters' the sacrament of their First Holy Communion, with Tammy standing in-between them. My step-daughter Emily is majoring in social service work, working for the rights of the young, elderly, and those with special needs. She continues to play a bit part of her sisters' lives, as she continues to live with us, keeping close with Hope and Faith. It's a wise financial decision on her behalf, and the girls love to have her around. She has her hands full, with school, assisting in overseeing the Sacred Heart Home for Orphans, next door; and still tends to them when she gets a chance. She is talking to one of the boys she has met in college, Timothy Johns. He seems to be a decent gentleman who attends mass regularly. I know that Emily wouldn't have it any other way. I continue to love my wife, who; after her ordeal in the birthing room is unable to give us any further children. I am grateful for Hope and Faith, and Emily too. I am the father of three beautiful daughters and a Father to my congregation as well. Tammy serves on the board for the Chairman, is the President of the CCW, and is one of those who get called upon for all kinds of work; from rosary making to washing dishes after funeral meals. She continues to make rosaries, along with Emily; and the girls are starting to pick up her techniques as well, as they have made everyone in the neighborhood a beaded bracelet, including one for me made from Job's tears. We live God's words, in our home and on our lips. I am blessed to be the only priest holding a position in the Personal Ordinariate of the Chair of St. Peter. He; St. Peter; himself was a married member of the clergy as the first pope, and I have prayed to him every day during the process, and to keep company with him every day. He has made a difference in our lives. As I do every day, I continue to pray that God keeps me here with this calling, as it is truly mine, and one of a kind. I am most grateful that I have paved the way for other priest who have completed protocol and have left the priesthood to make their way into the Ordinariate. I will continue to pray that God will continue to light our way. We need him in our lives, through our actions, thoughts and prayers. That reminds me, I need to continue to pray. I encourage you to pray along with me; please if you will.

Hail Mary, full of grace, the Lord is with thee; blessed are you among women, and blessed is the fruit of your womb, Jesus. Holy Mary, Mother of God, pray for us sinners, now and at the hour of our death. Amen

Hail Mary, full of grace, the Lord is with thee; blessed are you among women, and blessed is the fruit of your womb, Jesus. Holy Mary, Mother of God, pray for us sinners, now and at the hour of our death. Amen

Hail Holy Queen, Mother of Mercy! Our life, our sweetness, and our hope! To thee do we cry, poor banished children of Eve; to Thee do we send up our sighs, mourning and weeping in this valley of tears. Turn then, most gracious advocate, thine eyes of mercy toward us; and after this our exile show unto us the blessed fruit of thy womb Jesus; O clement, O loving, O sweet Virgin Mary.

Pray for us, O holy Mother of God

That we may be made worthy of the promises of Christ. Amen.

Oh God, whose only begotten Son, by His life, death, and resurrection has purchased for us the rewards of eternal life, grant that we beseech Thee, that meditating upon these mysteries in the most Holy Rosary of the Blessed Virgin Mary, we may imitate what they contain, and obtain what they promise: through the same, Christ our Lord. Amen.

Thank you for completing a rosary with me. It means a lot to have someone to pray it with.

Living a happy life is all that we can do on this earth. We are not perfect; so please don't expect yourself to be. On the other hand, please don't throw in the towel and ask for yours friends' permission to do things that The Lord would otherwise frown upon. I think that finding one's middle-ground, and understanding that, is our focal point. As we all try, we can fall. The wonderful part about this is that in/around your hometown Catholic Churches, you will find a confessional. That is a reminder that it is okay to not be perfect, and a reminder that he wants to give us forgiveness. All we need to do is ask. The Catholic obligation is once a month, for a confession, however, please go as often as is needed.

May God enrich your lives and your hearts. May He heal the 'broken sparrow' in you and in your life.